As soon as she moved his arm clamped down

The corridor was dark and cool and they were completely alone. There was no point in resisting.

"I thought I told you to stand still." Nicole shuddered, bitterly conscious of the caressing hand exploring the length of her body. "Take some well-meant advice, Nicole. Forget about Melanie. Enjoy your holiday. Don't make waves that could swamp everyone." He tightened his arm. "Are you listening?"

"Yes," she said with icy rage.

"A pity you cut your hair," Frazer murmured. "I liked it long. I used to fantasize about it... winding it around and around your neck like a silver collar. I could have strangled you with that hair."

Was that how he had killed his wife?

Books by Charlotte Lamb

A VIOLATION

HARLEQUIN PRESENTS

HARLEQUIN ROMANCES

These books may be available at your local bookseller.

For a free catalog listing all titles currently available, send your name and address to:

Harlequin Reader Service
P.O. Box 52040, Phoenix, AZ 85072-9988
Canadian address: Stratford, Ontario N5A 6W2

CHARLOTTE LAMB

darkness of the heart

Harlequin Books

TORONTO • NEW YORK • LONDON
AMSTERDAM • PARIS • SYDNEY • HAMBURG
STOCKHOLM • ATHENS • TOKYO • MILAN

Harlequin Presents first edition February 1984
ISBN 0-373-10668-8

Original hardcover edition published in 1983
by Mills & Boon Limited

CHAPTER ONE

THE spring night was chilly. March had come in like a lion, and was going out in very much the same way with gusts of wind and rain along the London streets, but when Nicole came out of the cinema she found that the sky had cleared and the rain had stopped. The wind still blew fiercely, whipping her blonde hair across her eyes as she turned homeward. She brushed it away as she walked, ignoring the sidelong look she got from a man in a prowling car.

'Want a lift, darling?' he called, keeping pace with her.

'Get lost,' said Nicole without turning her head. She ignored the next remark he made, which was extremely personal and probably impossible, and after a moment he drove off. Nicole walked faster, her hands buried in the pockets of her oxblood leather coat. Tomorrow she was going to tackle Sam on the subject of her long-overdue holiday. He would be difficult, he always was, but if she didn't take time off now while they weren't busy she wouldn't get another chance for months.

Turning a corner, she stopped in her tracks as she took in what was happening ahead of her. A group of struggling figures surged backward and forward on the pavement. It was hard to be sure what was happening at first, then she realised that one figure in a leather jacket was holding a man's arms yanked up behind him while another boy kicked and punched their victim.

Nicole began to run, her high-heeled boots ringing on the pavement. The victim stared desperately towards her.

'Help, get the police!'

The boy holding him grinned at Nicole over his shoulder. 'Don't you, lady, do yourself a favour—run on home and mind your own business.'

Laughing, the boy busy punching their victim turned to look at her, and at that second Nicole's hand chopped down sideways into his neck. He slumped to the ground without a murmur.

'God almighty!' the other boy muttered, his jaw dropping. Nicole turned towards him and he pushed aside the man he was gripping and began to run. Climbing on to a motorbike parked at the kerb, he started the throttle. The boy lying on the pavement crawled to his knees, making a whining sound. He just had time to stagger towards the kerb and get on to the pillion before the bike drove off, weaving from side to side.

Nicole watched it disappear, then turned to the victim. 'You okay?'

He was leaning on a gate, a hand pressed to his midriff, the sound of his breathing thick. 'I suppose so, thanks to you.' She couldn't see his face in the shadows. 'My God, that was the most amazing thing I've ever seen—what was it? Judo?'

'Trained self-defence.'

'Incredible!' He grimaced with pain, doubled up. 'I feel as if I've been put through a mangle.'

'We'd better ring the police,' said Nicole, brushing back short strands of fine silvery hair as the wind blew them across her face.

'I don't want any hassle,' he said, too quickly, and she

caught the gleam of his eyes, uneasiness in them. 'I'm not badly hurt and they didn't get anything. If we called the police what would I get but more aggravation. I didn't even have time to notice what those thugs looked like, the police wouldn't find them.' He was talking a good deal too fast and Nicole wasn't buying any of it, but she shrugged.

'Entirely up to you,' she said, swivelling to walk away, her leather coat flaring around the tight-fitting tan wool pants she wore. 'I should see a doctor tomorrow, all the same. You may have an internal injury—that was quite a beating you were taking.'

'Hey,' the man protested, catching her arm. 'Hang on, I haven't said thank you—can I offer you a drink? I need one pretty badly myself.'

'No, thanks, I rarely drink,' Nicole said, and smiled at him. 'Goodnight.'

He stared at her as she turned away again, gave a gasp.

'I know you!' he exclaimed, and Nicole looked quickly at him. 'Nicole,' he said. 'It is, isn't it? Nicole Lawton.'

Her face was expressionless, a poker player's watchfulness in her slanting green eyes.

'I don't believe it,' he said. 'My God, you've changed, but it is Nicole, I recognised you when you smiled. I'm Bevis Heaton, don't you remember me? You must remember me—good heavens, you were always at our house. You and Melanie were as thick as thieves, right from when you were in kindergarten together. I remember your hair vividly—it was marvellous, you used to wear it in one huge plait hanging right down your back, you could sit on it.'

'What a memory,' she said coolly, her hands in her coat pockets again.

'It must be years since I saw you,' he said. 'You were at Melanie's eighteenth birthday party, I remember you then—I was down from college and I kissed you in the garden and you hit me.' He began to laugh, and Nicole surveyed him with irony.

'Nice to know you remember,' she said drily.

'I remember everything from those days,' he said, sobering, his thin face becoming melancholy. 'Life isn't the same any more, is it? We used to have such fantastic times.' He looked up at the cold night sky, a sigh escaping from him. 'Everything was different, then.'

Nicole watched him, trying to reconcile the tall, wiry man with the boy she remembered—Bevis Heaton had been lanky, skinny, inclined to play the fool, rather highly strung under his noisy extrovert behaviour which, she had often felt, was assumed to cover an over-sensitive reaction to everything that happened to him. His emotions had always been too near the surface: he had had problems controlling them.

'Look,' he said impulsively, 'come in and have a drink, Nicole. I'll drive you home afterwards.'

'I'm sorry, I have a heavy day tomorrow,' she said politely. 'It was nice seeing you again, Bevis, but I must go.'

'Well, will you have dinner with me tomorrow? Oh, come on—after meeting again like this we can't just forget it. We have Melanie in common.' His words ended in another sigh, his face sombre. 'I can never believe it, can you? I often think, when the phone rings, that it will be her—crazy, I know. I suppose that's one of the ways we cope with these things.'

Nicole stared at him, frowning. 'What are you talking about?'

'Melanie,' he said, and then their eyes locked and for a moment they stared at each other, and Nicole's eyes widened and darkened as she read the expression on his face.

'Melanie?' she whispered.

He nodded slowly. 'I thought you knew—do you mean you hadn't heard? But it was two years ago, didn't anyone let you know?'

'Dead?' Nicole asked, although she already guessed the answer to the question, she just wanted to hear it said aloud so that she could force herself to believe it. Melanie, sparkling, alive, her beauty half composed of spirit; of the mobile vivacity of her small, heart-shaped face, her sudden, delighted laughter, her wildness and wilful, wayward determination to have her own way— how could Melanie stop living? The colour drained out of Nicole's face.

Bevis moved closer, put an arm around her tentatively as she caught at the gatepost. 'Are you okay, Nicole? You're white—it's a shock, isn't it? I know, I couldn't believe it either, I wouldn't believe it when I first heard! I thought it was some sort of mistake, they'd got the wrong girl—it couldn't be her, not Melanie.'

He had always been very close to his sister, who had been two years younger. Bevis had taken up a protective attitude to Melanie from an early age, partly, perhaps because their mother had died when they were young and the two children had been left alone a great deal by a busy father who had plenty of money to spend on them but very little time.

'Come in, have that drink,' Bevis invited. 'You look as if you need it—I know I do.'

Nicole was too dazed to argue this time. She let him

guide her up the path to the front door, her mind struggling to cope with the news she had just heard.

Bevis found his key, unlocked the front door and switched on the hall light. Nicole walked slowly into the house and he pushed open a door to the right and switched on the light in the room beyond. Nicole stood, looking around her; at the low, stone-coloured couch and matching Japanese-style armchairs, the deep blue carpet, the silky champagne-coloured wallpaper on which trailed Oriental flowers and birds in blues and pinks. There was a satinwood table beside the couch on which stood a few bottles of whisky and sherry. Nicole watched Bevis move over and pour two glasses of whisky.

He turned, holding one out to her. 'Sit down, Nicole—I'll switch on the electric fire, the house is quite chilly tonight.'

She silently took the glass and moved to the couch, sitting down with a feeling of relief. Her legs felt weak underneath her. She was very cold.

Bevis took off his coat and slung it over a chair, crossed to the hearth and switched on the large log-effect electric fire. He came back and stood in front of her, nursing his own glass for a second, then lifted it to his lips and swallowed half the contents rapidly.

She sipped her own whisky rather more slowly, grimacing at the taste. Tremors of shock ran through her, her skin was chill to touch as she brushed back a lock of hair from her cheek. She had a dozen questions to ask and couldn't phrase them.

At last she asked huskily: 'How did it happen? Was she ill?'

Bevis had been staring into his glass. Now he looked

up as though he had forgotten her presence, his eyes surprised and dark. 'She drowned,' he said shortly.

'Drowned?' Nicole winced as the word conjured up painful images. She sipped some more whisky, feeling Bevis staring at her, his gaze following the delicate, silvery strands which she wore loose, drifting around her face. The hairstyle was deliberate, it underlined the feminine fragility of her oval face—her misty almond-shaped green eyes with their long, darkened lashes, her high cheekbones, the vulnerable hollows beneath, the fine pale temples above her arched, pencilled brows— and it distracted the casual eye from features which contradicted that apparent delicacy. Her mouth was too wide, too firm; cool, with any suggestion of potential passion held tightly in control. Her jawline was taut, slightly aggressive, lifted almost arrogantly above her long, pale throat, and there was an arrogance, too, in the straight, finely chiselled nose.

'You've turned into quite a beauty,' Bevis told her, and she looked up and gave him a polite smile.

'Thank you.'

'You were a coltish girl, I remember, always loping about on long, thin legs in shorts.'

'Only in summer,' Nicole said drily.

He made a wry face. 'It always seemed to be summer—I barely remember any of the winters.'

'How did it happen?' Nicole asked suddenly, breaking into the words. 'Melanie could always swim like a fish, I used to envy her, she could outswim anyone in the class—did she take some stupid risk?' That was the sort of idiocy she could imagine from Melanie, who had loved to show off, diving always from the topmost board, swimming underwater for so long she was gasping for breath when she did surface and when they were down by the sea, swimming far out from the shore, further than anyone else. It always had to be more than anyone else for Melanie, she wanted to do more, have more, be more than any of them.

Bevis had flushed suddenly, a dark, ugly stain running over his cheeks, his eyes had flecks of red in them. 'That was what I said when they told me—how could it have happened? The sea was as calm as a millpond the night she died. I asked about the weather, and they had to admit it had been so warm you couldn't bear to sleep indoors, there wasn't a breath of wind, not a ripple on the sea. She was sleeping out on a beach because it was so hot. They said she must have got cramp, swimming to cool off—like hell she did!' he burst out with a flare of angry aggression, as though Nicole had argued with him, glaring at her. 'Like hell!'

'Where was this?'

'Greece,' said Bevis.

'Greece?' Nicole felt a little shock of surprise, her voice rising. She watched Bevis drain his glass, his head tilted back, his eyes almost closed as he swallowed, and saw a dark shadow beneath his brown eyes. Looking at him intently she saw that what she had taken for the look of maturity had been as much the shadow of unhappiness. Bevis was not merely an adult, his face was worn, hollowed with grief. He and Melanie had been so close, almost twins in their constant devotion, their love for each other's company. Her loss would have had a traumatic effect on him. 'What was she doing in Greece?'

'They'd been living there,' Bevis told her. 'For a couple of years.' He walked over to refill his glass after a glance at Nicole's barely touched whisky. Over his shoulder he asked: 'Were you at the wedding? I don't remember.'

'No,' Nicole said shortly, her eyes lowered.

'She married a journalist, Frazer Holt—he was working in Fleet Street then, but he wrote a book which was a best-seller and gave up his job to write full-time. He's written a couple since, they sell well—God knows why, I can't read them, they bore me stiff, but he makes a bomb.' He turned and came back, leaned on the hearth looking down at the glowing fire, and in profile in that light she could see even more clearly how tired and ill he looked. 'He took her off to Greece, to a little island miles from anywhere. Mel was bored out of her skull. She hated it, she liked living in London, she didn't want to live on some godforsaken place miles from everything she knew.'

Nicole stared at her fingers pressed around the glass, the pads showing white with every whorl thrown into prominence under that pressure. 'She had *him*, though; her husband.' Her throat was dry, she cleared briefly. 'Weren't they happy?'

Bevis laughed in an ugly way, his mouth stiff, and Nicole looked up at him, stared at him, wishing she could read his mind.

'I could tell you a thing or two,' he said, then stopped short. 'I've been warned off, I'd better not open my mouth.'

'Warned off? By whom? About what?' Her voice sharpened, her eyes even more intent. She was used to using her intuition about people, guessing at unsaid feelings, hidden motives. Bevis could not have changed that much in the eight years since she last remembered meeting him. The more she studied him the more she could connect the unhappy man standing there with the highly strung boy she had known so well years ago.

She watched the hesitation in his face, saw him struggle with himself, then it burst out of him and she saw that these thoughts had been occupying his mind for a long, long time. They had been obsessing him, preying on him; his voice had a thickened force as he spoke which told of a deep, ungovernable emotion. 'It was all hushed up, I can't prove it was all lies. I tried, but I didn't get anywhere. He's a rich man, he can afford to buy people off, and those he didn't buy were frightened to talk.' He came over and stood in front of her, flushed and distraught, talked at her rather than to her. 'Did you ever meet him? Oh, yes, you must have done—sometimes I get so confused.'

Nicole didn't answer. The memory of Frazer Holt was burnt too deeply into her own mind; she couldn't talk about him to Bevis, but he probably wouldn't have listened anyway, he was too caught up with his own feelings.

'He was jealous, of course—every man who met Melanie fell for her. Do you remember what she was like at eighteen?'

'Very well,' Nicole said drily, and he gave her a wistful smile.

'Beautiful, wasn't she? Men took one look and dropped like flies. She only had to smile at them. You could watch their faces, it used to make me laugh to see them staring. Holt didn't laugh, though. He hated the effect she had on other men. He wanted her all to himself.'

Nicole picked up her glass again and drank to cover her own reaction to that last remark. She was very pale.

'That's why he took her off to this Greek island. He wrote all day, but Mel had nothing to do but look at the seagulls and sunbathe. She went spare. It wasn't so bad in the summer—tourists came and she could have some fun, but the winters were a drag. She told him she was going back to England, and Holt said he'd kill her if she tried.' Bevis looked at Nicole with shadowy eyes, and she got the impression he was on the point of tears, his mouth was trembling. 'I didn't believe her. She told me what he'd threatened and I laughed it off. Take no notice, I said to her, he's just bluffing. He didn't mean it, it was all talk. Leave him, I said, come home where you belong.' His voice roughened and he stopped, then said: 'Two months later she was dead.' His face working violently, he turned and walked away, stood with his back to her. Nicole watched him, her eyes sombre.

'I hired a private detective from Athens to go there and see if he could prove what really happened,' Bevis told her. 'He went, I got one report from him, then he suddenly wired me that he wasn't going on with the case. There was nothing wrong, he told me. Her death had been an accidental drowning, there were no suspicious circumstances.'

'Did you go out there yourself?'

Bevis turned. He had himself under control now. 'I went for the funeral, but I got nowhere when I tried to ask questions. None of the locals would talk to me. I don't speak Greek and they all pretended not to speak English. The local police were sympathetic but pretended to think I was out of my mind with grief when I said Melanie didn't die by accident.'

Nicole nodded without saying anything, sure that, in their place, she would have come to the same conclusion. You only had to look at that tense, almost neurotic face to suspect that Bevis was not someone on whose views you could rely.

'Holt knew I'd sent the man from Athens. He wrote to me and told me I was wasting my time and money, there was nothing to find out.' Bevis grimaced at her. 'Notice, he didn't say I was wrong—he just warned me off, he said I'd only destroy myself if I went on dwelling on the past, I should forget about it, accept that she was dead and . . .' He made a wild gesture. 'The bastard was threatening me, he didn't even try to hide it!'

'Had you used a reputable agency in Athens?' Nicole asked, and he looked at her blankly, then shrugged and nodded.

'Oh, yes, yes, I got my lawyer to find out a good firm.'

'Who were they?'

Bevis frowned irritably. 'Oh, I forget the name . . .' He stopped, looked at her sharply. 'Why? Do you know anything about detective agencies?'

'I thought I might have heard of them,' Nicole said evasively.

'What do you do now, Nicole?' Bevis glanced down at her hands. 'Not married, I see?'

'No,' she said, half smiling.

'What sort of job do you do?'

'I'm in insurance,' she said, and he looked at her politely.

'Really?'

Nicole smiled fully, her green eyes mischievous. 'It's always a conversation stopper,' she said. 'Dull, I'm afraid.'

'Oh, well,' Bevis said tolerantly. 'Pays well, I suppose?'

'Yes,' she said with irony. 'Yes, it pays well.'

He returned to his obsession. 'You must know how I feel—you were her best friend. Mel loved you, you were always together, did everything together until . . .'

'Yes,' said Nicole, interrupting. 'We were good friends until she married.' She got up. 'I must go, Bevis. It's well past one and I'm very tired. I'm very sorry about Melanie, it's tragic.' She held out her hand and he took it, staring at her.

'Must you . . .'

'Yes, really, I'm very sleepy.' .

'I haven't thanked you yet—you may have saved my life.'

'Nonsense, they wouldn't have killed you.' Nicole looked at him directly. 'Did you know them, Bevis?'

'Know . . . no, of course not,' he said, flushing, and she knew he lied from the selfconscious voice, the restless sideways movement of the eyes.

'Because if you did, and they were bothering you, you'd be wise to go to the police.'

'They were just muggers,' Bevis said. 'Happens all the time in London these days, the streets aren't as safe as they used to be, especially around here. Do you live near here, Nicole?'

'Ermine Street,' she said. 'I have a flat on the ground floor of Number Seven.' She walked to the door and Bevis followed close on her heels. In the hall he put a hand on her arm.

'Thanks, all the same—I must obviously learn some judo.'

'You must,' she agreed. 'You never know when it might come in useful.'

He forced a smile. 'And you're so beautiful, too—

who'd have thought it? I'll never forget their faces, they were staggered. So was I! It made me feel pretty stupid, I can tell you.'

'No reason why it should. I'm trained, you're not.' She opened the front door. 'Goodnight, Bevis.'

'Look, could we have dinner some time? Having met you again, I'd like to see you, talk over old times.'

She smiled. 'I'd love to some time, but I'm just going away on holiday—I'll be away for a few weeks. Give me a ring, I'm in the book.' She wasn't, her number was ex-directory, but she did not want to have an embarrassing scene with him. She had been quite fond of Bevis years ago, but time had altered both of them and they had nothing in common but a past Nicole preferred to forget.

She walked down the path, aware of him in the lighted doorway, watching her, gave him a brief wave and vanished into the shadowy night.

It only took her five minutes to cover the rest of the way to her flat, and while she was walking she thought, not about Melanie, but deliberately about the attack on Bevis which she had foiled. She had the distinct impression he had been nervous about the police being called in; there had been a wary look about him. It had not surprised her when he asked her not to report the incident. Perhaps Bevis had known the two boys, perhaps he had been expecting the attack. It was impossible to say what was behind his reluctance to have the police involved, but there was more to the incident than met the eye. All Nicole's instincts told her that. Bevis had lied—by omission if not directly. It was none of her business, and Nicole had let it pass without comment, but it had aroused her curiosity.

been by their ordeal out at the cliffs. Michael could only hope that was the case.

He watched as Steven motioned to the tray, silently offering to make her another one, but Nikki shrugged him off. She'd gotten what she wanted, the opportunity to *take* without asking.

Michael had learned over the years that Nikki rarely accepted anything that was offered. She preferred to step in and grab what she wanted. Control was the issue with Nikki and she knew she could take with ease from Steven.

"As hard as it is to be cooped up here, complaining isn't going to get us anywhere," Gracie said softly. "We can't change the weather. We just need to be patient."

"Shut up, Gracie," Nikki snapped. "No one was talking to you."

From the corner of his eye, Michael saw Kylie lean forward. Her facial expression was protective. She wasn't happy with Nikki's attack. "Back off, Nikki. Gracie's just telling it like it is. Right now we're all tired and irritable. We need to make a concentrated effort to get along."

"Oh goodie, little peacemaker Kylie McKee has stepped up to the plate," Nikki retorted. "Come on, show us what you've got."

"What I've got is a splitting headache." Kylie stood up. "If you'll all excuse me, I think I've sat through enough."

She headed for the door.

"Going so soon?" Nikki said with exaggerated sweetness, her eyes narrowing. "Don't run off. We've hardly gotten started."

"All right, let's everyone settle down," Michael said. "Nikki's just mouthing off, Kylie. Ignore her, that's what taken up her usual position next to him, her body pressed in close, trying to share the most intimate space possible.

In contrast, Kylie was seated as far away from him as she could. If she could have retreated to her father's cabin, he was pretty sure that's where she'd be at the moment.

"What's the word on the storm?" Leslie asked from her position near the bar. From the looks of her, Michael figured she was already three sheets to the wind.

"Any chance we're going to be able to get out of here anytime soon?" she asked.

Steven snagged a sliver of toast off the silver tray on the coffee table and ladled a healthy scoop of Beluga caviar onto the center. He sat back. "I was listening to the short-wave a while ago. The low has stalled right over us, but they think there might be some let up tomorrow. Can't say for sure."

"Wonderful, I think if I have to spend another day in this hell hole, I'm going to go stark raving mad." Nikki reached over and snagged the toast point out of Steven's hand, popping it into her mouth.

She grinned wickedly and then winked, the dazzle of her smile meant to take the sting out of her antics. As always, Steven accepted her behavior without protest. But then, Steven had always put up with Nikki. The guy had been in love with her for about as long as Michael could remember. Not that Nikki would ever give him the time of day.

A touch of something, regret maybe, possibly fear, slid across Nikki's face. Her hands shook slightly as she brushed a few remaining crumbs off them. Perhaps she was more shaken up than she was willing to admit, showing a bit of bravado in an attempt to cover up how affected she'd

She let herself into her flat very quietly. The house was silent and dark. She switched on the light in her sitting-room and looked around her with a sigh of weariness. Now that she was home and could go to bed she knew she no longer felt tired mentally, although her body felt heavy and slack after a very long, hard day. She went into the bathroom and stripped, then stepped under the shower, feeling the warm spray of water hitting her cold skin as she began to wash. She closed her eyes and let the soap wash off under the shower, her face lifted towards the jet of water. Behind her lowered lids a face floated: dark, powerful, hard-boned. Nicole hurriedly opened her eyes and stepped out of the cubicle. A wave of heat had swept up her body. She grabbed down a towelling robe and huddled into it, tying the belt tightly around her slender waist. In the bathroom mirror her features floated mistily on the steamed glass, her hair hung in damp coils around her face.

She padded down the hall into her kitchen and made herself some cocoa, taking a couple of aspirins with a glass of water while she waited for the milk to heat. Her head was pounding, her eyes felt sore and hot, as though she was about to have a bout of 'flu.

She went to bed in that dead, chill middle of the night when nothing stirs and it seems as if day will never come. Her bed felt cold; she curled into a foetal position on her side, her knees up, trying to relax, to sleep. She could do neither. She kept hearing Bevis say: 'He killed her . . .' She kept seeing a dark, angry face; deep, deep blue eyes, searingly bright and fierce.

Some of what Bevis had told her hadn't surprised her. Nicole could well imagine circumstances in which Frazer Holt might kill. He was that sort of man—a man to be wary of, to steer clear of if you had any sense, one who could face danger without flinching and who enjoyed the risk of sailing close to the wind.

Melanie must have been fascinated by him from the day she first met him, even before that, probably, when she had only heard about him. Nicole might have realised what would happen if she had been thinking straight, but her own emotions had been too clouded. It hadn't occurred to her that Melanie would be excited by the aura of danger he carried around with him.

Of course, she should have guessed; she knew Melanie, she had known her for most of her life. Nicole was quite good now at working out other people's motives and probable reactions. Melanie never had been able to do that. She had been too self-obsessed, she saw nothing outside herself, dazzled by her own reflection. If she had not been so blind, she might have realised that Frazer Holt was not a man who would stand for being made to look a fool, to him that would be unforgivable.

She might have realised, too, how Nicole would take the news that Melanie was marrying Frazer. She had stood there, smiling, and Nicole had stared at her in frozen silence, fighting with things she could not allow herself to say, with feelings she would not allow herself to reveal. Melanie had been all sunshine, glittering with triumph and self-congratulation.

'I want you to be my bridesmaid,' she had said.

'No!' Nicole had broken out, the word hot and harsh, wrenched from her very depths.

Melanie's eyes had rounded, widened, all innocence. 'But, Nicky, why? Of course you must, we always said . . .'

'No,' Nicole had said again, but with more control,

gritting her teeth to keep everything in, her hands curled at her sides with the nails digging into her palms.

Later she had stood in front of a mirror and looked at herself with loathing. Bevis had remembered her too clearly. She remembered herself exactly that way—her body image had been deplorable at that age, she had hated looking into mirrors. She had been too aware of her height, her incredibly long thin legs. When she was a schoolgirl someone had nicknamed her the Stork, and it had stung, but it had made her even more selfconscious. While Melanie was small, and curvy and sexy, Nicole had been gawky and uncontrolled, her long plait emphasising her youth, her too-wide mouth seeming to her to obliterate the chance of beauty.

She had not merely despised her own looks that day, she had despised her feelings. At nineteen, she had been ashamed of her own capacity to feel emotion, she had been afraid of it, aware that it could flare out with the raw crudity of a jet of natural gas from the ground, hating that, just as she hated knowing that her movements had an uncontrolled jerkiness at times, she lacked grace and co-ordination.

In the years since that day she had taught herself the control she had lacked during her teens, but the news of Melanie's death had shaken her to her depths. Even hatred wears out in the end, and death is so final—the bitter silence between herself and Melanie would never now be broken.

She slept fitfully all night, waking up from dreams with a smothered cry several times, to lie in the dark and think about Melanie. In the morning there were dark shadows under her eyes.

She got to her office at half past nine, made several

phone calls and then went into her boss's office to find him up to his neck in huge law books.

'Sam, I'm going on holiday,' she announced, and he looked up, scowling.

'Don't start that again, I can't spare you—I'm lunching with Partington today. He says he has a new case for you.'

'I'm leaving tomorrow,' said Nicole, ignoring that. Sam never took a holiday himself these days, apart from his annual two weeks with his sister in Lyme Regis which was, she had gathered over the years, more of a penance than a holiday, since Sam and his sister detested each other cordially. When she had been foolish enough to ask him why, in that case, he always went down to stay with his sister for a fortnight each year, Sam had stared at her with his round, owlish eyes wide and said: 'She *is* my sister, blood's thicker than water.'

'This is our busy time,' he said now.

'It always is—I haven't had any time off for nine months, and I'm going sailing.'

Sam looked at the grey sky stretching beyond the window and laughed. 'In this weather? Are you crazy?'

'Not around England,' Nicole said. 'I'm going in search of blue skies and some sun. I've hired a boat for two weeks and booked a flight for tomorrow morning.'

'What about Partington?'

'Ask him to wait, or start the job yourself and I'll pick it up when I get back.'

Sam flung himself backward in his battered old leather chair, his hands behind his head. He was a short, sturdy man with a balding head and brown eyes which could be as hard as stones or melt with amusement and warmth. His mind was as sharp as a knife, his intuition quick and shrewd. Before he founded a private detective agency, he had worked at Scotland Yard for fifteen years. Nicole's father had been his best friend, they had been partners in the police force as young men and after Sam resigned to work privately Joe Lawton had kept in touch until he died. As a little girl, Nicole had called him Uncle Sam, now she dropped the Uncle, although for eleven years Sam had been all the family she knew. When she first suggested joining his agency, Sam had laughed.

'You? You're crazy, it isn't a job for girls!' he had said, but Nicole had worn him down gradually.

'Water dropping on a stone,' he had groaned. 'The Chinese water torture . . . heaven preserve me from scheming females, I must be nuts to consider it!' Then he had looked at her and said: 'Okay, okay, we'll give it a trial run, but if you find the going too rough, I want you to have the guts to admit it and quit before you get hurt.'

Nicole had promised eagerly, sure from the start that it was what she wanted to do. Sam had got used to confiding in her, talking freely to her about his cases, unaware that her fascinated attention sprang from a desire to do the work herself. Nicole had the sort of mind which can focus intently on a problem: ferret away for months, carefully sift through confusing material, fasten on tiny nuggets of fact, add them together slowly, piece by piece, until the apparently haphazard picture became clear and concrete.

The agency employed a staff of eight, now, although the bulk of the work was still done by Sam and Nicole. They were successful and respected, they were highly paid specialists who had won their reputation by hard work and reliable results.

'Where are you planning on going?' he asked her now.

'Greece,' Nicole said.

Sam considered that, nodding. 'Sailing around the islands? Do you remember that summer we had . . .'

'Yes,' she said, smiling at him. Sam had taught her to sail, just as he had taught her to shoot, to fence, to ride, and one of their most memorable holidays during her childhood had been spent with her parents and Sam sailing around the Cyclades, calling in at scattered little islands for a day before sailing on to find somewhere new. Nicole's memory of those weeks had a clarity and beauty she recalled with enormous pleasure—blue sea, blue skies, a fresh crisp wind and a light which was almost unearthly in its radiance, conferring on everything you saw an intensity of reality. That mountain peak, that white-winged gull, seemed the first ever in the history of the world, everything seemed newly minted, vividly alive.

Sam sighed. 'Well, take care,' he said. 'Don't take any risks.'

'I won't,' she promised, and went over to kiss the top of his head.

Sam wriggled away. He disliked demonstrations of affection. 'Get off,' he muttered. 'I'm busy—clear your desk before you go off tonight, I don't want any loose ends hanging around while you're away.'

'Sam, you're in a class of your own,' Nicole mocked, and went out, smiling.

She hadn't had any trouble finding out where Frazer Holt was living—all she had to do was ring a contact on a national newspaper and within five minutes she knew where to find Frazer. Later that morning, her contact rang back to read her everything he had dug up on

Melanie's death—it wasn't much, just the bare facts, more or less as Bevis had given them to her.

'Why the interest?' her contact asked. 'Anything in it for me? Is there something more than that?'

'No,' Nicole said cautiously. 'I'm working on a line which happened to cross this one, that's all.' She knew better than to imply anything which might lead to a libel case. Frazer Holt was a public name now, a famous man with money and a reputation. If she made any mistakes she could find herself in legal trouble.

'If you do run across anything . . .'

'I know, you'll be the first to hear,' she promised. It was the price of the information she had got so rapidly, tit for tat was the name of the game. 'Don't worry, I'll owe you one,' she said as she rang off.

She spent the next night in Greece, at a hotel near Piraeus, her windows wide open to let the warm air circulate around the stuffy little room. Below lay Microlimano Bay, a huddle of restaurants hugging the shoreline, still crowded late in the evening, with people dining outside as well as in, the sound of bouzouki music floating up towards her open window until well into the middle of the night.

She woke several times from dreams of Melanie, shuddering. From the minute she heard that Melanie was dead, her mind had been eaten alive with questions, and Nicole could never bear to live with unanswered questions.

She had shut her mind to thoughts of Melanie and Frazer for years, she had told herself all that part of her life was finished, forgotten, but she knew she had been lying to herself. They had left a barbed hook inside her, and although a skin had grown over it, disguising it even from Nicole herself, the news of Melanie's death had ripped away that uneasy bandage and she felt the ache of the barb again.

The following morning she was up at dawn. She left Piraeus an hour later, setting course for Mykonos. The wind was light and cool, the sea glittered ahead of her like a broken mirror; blue and silver, the sky arching overhead, cloudless, calm, halcyon. Her blonde hair streamed back from her face, rippling and stirring, as she moved around the boat, and she got a wave and a shout: '*Kalimera*!' from two men on a small fishing boat which passed with a trail of gulls in its wake. She called back, smiled, watching the birds hanging with spread wings on the current of warm air from the ship.

Nicole had brought some food with her—fruit and fetta cheese and boiled eggs, a flat loaf of bread in the traditional Greek shape, as big as a dinner plate, slightly domed in the centre. She had some bottles of water and some coffee in a flask. She was in no hurry to reach Mykonos, the weather was too good and it was fantastic to sail at your leisure on that sleek sea with nothing to do but enjoy yourself. In shorts and a t-shirt she clambered around, sat back and watched the creaming wake along the side, felt the sun warming her arms and legs, making her face glow. She would have liked to sail on for ever in this golden light—ahead of her lay an experience she was going to find painful and disturbing.

It might have been wiser to accept the news of Melanie's death, mourn briefly for the old affection which had ended so badly, and forget all about it, but Nicole could not do that. That was why she did the job she did—she had a passion for uncovering the truth, however painful.

It was sunset when she finally approached the little island. From far away she could see it: white geometric blocks glittering in the dying light, a crescent of flat-roofed little houses crammed together along a curving bay, and behind them stark, rocky hillsides rising to meet the blue sky which was darkening slowly.

As she skimmed closer she saw the backs of houses seeming almost to grow out of the sea, climbing up out of the waves, like strange sea flowers, and as lights came on in the little town they gleamed on the waters; pink and yellow and green, streaking and shimmering as the waves washed to and fro on the rocky foreshore, conferring an air of mystery on the sea itself.

Nicole steered her way into the tiny harbour where a few men stood gossiping in the twilight among the weighted nets and coils of rope. They stared at her expressionlessly, brown weathered faces lined and wrinkled, dark eyes, windblown hair, then through them darted a boy in a white shirt and dusty black jeans. He held out his hand, smiling, and Nicole tossed him the rope she held, watched him tie up with a deft, accustomed speed.

One of the men watching said something and the others all laughed. Reaching out a hand, the man ruffled the boy's black hair. 'Eh, Adoni?' he mocked, and the boy shrugged his hand off, but laughed.

Nicole gathered up her belongings and climbed on to the quayside. Her gaze moved over the whitewashed houses huddled below the hills. Somewhere in those twisting, meandering streets lived Frazer Holt, and tomorrow she must find him, but for tonight she wanted to reach the hotel at which she had booked by telephone from Athens. She was tired and grubby, her skin sunburnt and windburnt, she needed a shower and she needed a meal.

'*Kalimera*,' she said to the boy Adoni as he stood watching her, his lustrous dark eyes interested and amused.

'*Kalimera, kyria*,' he said, and smiled.

'Hotel Delos?' she asked, looking up at the buildings which began just a few yards away.

The boy nodded, reached out and took her bag from her hand. 'Please,' he said. 'English?'

Nicole smiled, nodding. How old was he? she wondered, watching his olive-skinned face. Ten? Eleven? He had an impish smile, his teeth faintly crooked, his dark eyes lustrous, filled with a strange mixture of shrewd sophistication and innocence.

'I speak,' he informed her, nodding. 'Please, come.'

The men lounging on the quayside were inspecting her boat with interest, but they turned to watch as she followed the boy towards a building a stone's throw from the waterfront.

'I, Adoni,' the boy said over his shoulder.

'Hallo, Adoni,' said Nicole. 'I am Nicole.'

He stopped, grinning, and she held out her hand. Gravely, he shook it. 'Please,' he said, 'you must be permitted.'

Nicole surveyed him, her brows rising. 'Permitted?'

He gestured towards the building outside which they had halted. She stared blankly and Adoni searched for some more of his careful English. He gestured to her boat, then back to the building. 'Permitted,' he said, smiling. 'You must be permitted—you have drachmas?'

'Oh, I get you,' said Nicole, starting to laugh. 'I need permission to bring my boat into Mykonos?'

He nodded, beaming with relief at having got through to her, then led the way to where the port official was waiting. Nicole realised, as she shook hands with the weathered old man, that she had already seen him on the quayside. He must have darted off to don his official personality while Adoni was explaining.

Adoni dealt with the business matter rapidly. He talked for her and Nicole handed over her harbour fee with a smile, then followed Adoni into the network of narrow streets which curved and curled and wandered in and out of each other, confusing and disorientating her. They never seemed to arrive anywhere: followed first one and then another, as if in a maze. Now and then she caught sight of the waterfront between the white houses; the cafés were lit with garish yellow lights and men sat at the tables, drinking, behind their heads the sky turning a dusky mauve shot with gold and pink.

At last Adoni put a hand under her elbow in formal courtesy. 'Please, miss, Hotel Delos.'

She followed him through the glass door into a shadowy lobby. On a counter stood a dim lamp which formed a small circle of light by which she saw the woman standing to welcome her. Beyond clustered several children who stared, dark-eyed and yet oddly polite without smiling.

Adoni broke into his rapid, husky Greek and the woman nodded and pushed a large book across the counter. 'Please, miss,' Adoni said. 'To sign.'

Nicole signed her name. Adoni and the woman studied it. Nicole produced her passport, they studied that. They smiled at her.

'Please, miss, to come,' said Adoni. 'I bring bag.'

Nicole followed up the stairs to a small, clean room on

the first floor and Adoni carefully placed her bag on the chair by the bed. Nicole found some money and handed it to him with a smile. He beamed, the money vanished.

'My name is Nicole,' she told him again, smiling.

'See you, Nicole,' Adoni said in sudden, comic American, and disappeared. The woman laughed and winked at Nicole. She seemed pleased to have a visitor—it was early in the season, Mykonos was a small island, and almost empty at this time of year as the great cruise ships had not yet begun to sail the Greek island routes.

'If there is anything you need, *kyria*, please call me on the telephone,' the receptionist said in thick-accented English. 'I am Irena Vourlamis.'

'Thank you, Irena,' said Nicole. 'What time is dinner?'

'Whenever you wish,' Irena said, and a moment later Nicole was alone, standing by the window looking down into the shadowy street and hearing the waves breaking on the rocks somewhere beyond the houses. The bedside lamp lent a soft glow to the room behind her and, with the shutters open and the window wide, moths began to flutter softly past her face. She was reluctant to move; she felt tranced, bewitched by the spell of the place, like someone trapped in a sea-shell, the crustacean town embedding her, curving endlessly around her, with the sound of the sea always in her ears.

She broke away with an effort, showered, brushed her damp hair and dressed in a light cotton dress, sleeveless and simple, the skirt very short and softly pleated. White, unadorned, it looked Grecian, although she had bought it to play tennis on summer evenings. Standing by the window, brushing her hair with the evening wind blowing through the silvery strands, she watched a few people walk past in an unhurried way. A church bell began to clang somewhere, birds were making sleepy evening calls on the flat rooftops around her, a bouzouki began to play in a taverna down the street.

A man turned the corner and strolled along in the shadows. Nicole watched him idly, then her whole body jerked to attention, her pulse picked up and began to thunder.

He was unaware of being watched; his long-limbed body moving at a stride, thick black hair blowing back from a tanned face. Nicole stared, her senses drinking in every detail of his appearance. He had changed, but then what else had she expected? He was spare and lean, his broad shoulders more muscular under the thin white shirt he wore, open at the neck and showing her the power of his brown throat. In profile he had a hard arrogance she did not remember so strongly. She could not see the blue eyes, they were veiled by lowered lids as he stared ahead.

He was gone a second later. She stood staring at the while wall opposite as though it was incised with his clearcut profile, the shadow also engraved on her inner vision. Her hands closed over the sill, a stab of pain, of fear, going through her. Had she been wise to come?

CHAPTER TWO

It was several minutes before she was sufficiently in control to move away from the window and go down to find Irena Vourlamis. As she came down the stairs a child scuttled away out of sight, then a moment later Irena appeared, and Nicole smiled at her.

'You are hungry now?' Irena asked. Slightly built, olive-skinned, she had black eyes and hair and a calm, thin face. When she spoke slowly she was perfectly comprehensible, but as soon as she became excited, Nicole came to realise, Irena's accent thickened and made her words hard to follow.

'Very hungry,' Nicole agreed. Sea air and exercise had given her an appetite.

'We are eating now,' said Irena with obvious hesitation. 'If you like, you can eat with us or I can serve you in the small dining-room.' She looked at Nicole uncertainly. 'You are the only guest.'

'I'd love to eat with you,' Nicole said, and heard the other woman give a half-stifled sigh of relief. Nicole followed her into the back of the hotel. In a small family sitting-room the children sat around a table talking in Greek. Their voices broke off as Nicole followed their mother into the room. Irena gestured to a place at the end of the table.

'Please, sit,' she said, and Nicole obeyed, giving the dark-eyed children a quick look and a smile.

'I'm Nicole,' she said, and waited while they looked at

32

their mother and then at each other.

'They do not speak English yet,' Irena said with amusement. 'The eldest is Spiro, then there is Elena, then my baby, Demetrius.'

In turn they smiled shyly as their names were pronounced, nodding. Irena filled a large soup plate from a tureen and it was handed down to Nicole, who inhaled the savoury odour of the soup, distinguishing the scents of lemon and thyme.

'Bread?' Irena asked, offering her a wicker basket.

'Thank you.' Nicole took a slice of the loose-weaved yellowish local bread, wondering if Irena was a widow, since there was no sign of a man about the hotel.

The meal was a simple one; after the delicately flavoured soup came a dish of local-caught red snapper, a rather bony fish, cooked with onions and peppers, with which Irena served a large bowl of green salad, sprinkled with white fetta cheese.

As if guessing at Nicole's curiosity, Irena told her while they ate that her husband, Paul, was a fisherman but was off at the moment fishing somewhere among the islands. 'He may be home tomorrow,' Irena said, shrugging. 'I hope . . .' Her smile was wry, amused.

Nicole smiled back. 'Your English is very good—where did you learn it? Here on Mykonos?'

Irena shook her head. 'In Athens—I started to learn English at the University before I was married. Once I meant to be an archaeologist, but when I met Paul . . .' She laughed, looked at the children. 'No more study,' she said, without apparent regret.

'Did you meet your husband in Athens?'

'No, I met his brother,' Irena said, and laughed. 'Georgi Vourlamis was studying archaeology too, you know? Like me, he needed money.' She made a face. 'We're not rich people, you know? Georgi still can't afford to get married. Well, Georgi said to me that I should come to Mykonos and work as a guide with him one summer. I came and I met Paul and married him.' She shrugged, smiling. 'And that was that.'

'Was Georgi's heart broken?' Nicole asked, laughing, and Irena gave her a quick, blank look, obviously not amused, so Nicole hurriedly said: 'How useful to speak some English when you run a hotel here. Are there many English people on Mykonos now?' She kept her voice casual and helped herself to more salad as she spoke; it had a delicious clean taste of lemon juice and olive oil.

'One or two in the new villas up the hill above the town. There is much new building here lately, many new faces.'

'Isn't there a famous writer living here?'

Irena's hand stopped on its way to her mouth, Nicole saw it tremble slightly and some flakes of fish fell from the fork.

'Many Greek writers come here,' Irena said after a moment.

'I was told an English writer lived here, I heard something about him in Athens.' Nicole watched the other woman intently. She must have heard of Frazer Holt; he was too famous for her to be unaware that he lived on Mykonos. The island was far too small for one of its residents to escape notice, especially a best-selling writer.

'What did you hear in Athens?' Irena asked, her Greek accent suddenly becoming much thicker again. 'Who is this writer?'

'I think his name was Holt,' said Nicole, her green eyes sharp. 'In Athens they said something about his wife . . . did she get killed or something like that?' Irena's blank stare puzzled her; why was she so wary and unforthcoming?

Irena's mouth formed a wry pout. 'Oh, in Athens, they tell you anything!' She offered Nicole the copper jug of local white wine. 'Please, some more!'

Nicole stifled a yawn, apologised with a smile. 'I am very tired—it has been a long day, I left Pireaus at first light, and all that sea air and sunshine has made me sleepy. The wine helped,' she added, laughing. 'It's very good, but I mustn't drink any more, thank you. I shall sleep like a log as it is.'

'Some coffee?' Irena suggested, getting up. 'I can make you Greek coffee, or there is instant coffee?'

'Greek will be fine, thank you.'

Irena went out and the children got down and began clearing the table, refusing Nicole's offer of help with smiles and shrugs. The small room opened out on a shadowy alleyway, the door standing open and admitting the scent of warm dust and flowers. A scrawny-flanked little black cat slunk into the room, paused on seeing Nicole and watched her with nervous, green-gleaming eyes. Nicole leant over and picked up a plate on which lay some fish scraps. Irena came back as she was feeding them to the cat, and clicked her tongue.

'You must not encourage them, they are everywhere. We won't get rid of her for days now.' Her voice was tart and impatient.

'I'm sorry,' Nicole apologised. 'She looked so hungry.'

'Oh, there are always fish heads to be picked up on the quay.' Irena placed a small cup of thick, muddy coffee in front of her and Nicole sipped the sweet liquid, hearing the children laughing as they washed up in the next room, their murmurs and the running of water, the clatter of plates, soporific in the half-light of the warm room. From somewhere near by she heard deeper, male voices, and further off, the whisper of the sea on the rocky coast. Her body was heavy with that pleasant weariness which follows physical exertion in the open air. She thought with lazy anticipation of her narrow white bed in the quiet room upstairs. She was going to sleep for twelve hours at a stretch. She was reluctant to move yet; to get up and break the spell of the soft, night sounds which were lulling her senses to rest.

When she did walk slowly upstairs she found that her muscles were aching. It was ages since she had spent a day sailing; it kept you at a stretch, always watchful, when you're handling a boat on your own you can never relax for long. In her room she undressed and washed, then slid into bed, her eyes closing almost as soon as her head had touched the pillow. Tomorrow would be soon enough to cope with thoughts of Frazer Holt, tonight she wanted some uninterrupted sleep.

When the door was flung open Nicole struggled up on one elbow; blinking dazedly as the light snapped on, her sleepy eyes trying to focus on the man who had come into the room.

'Who are you?' she asked, instinctively pulling herself together and starting to think even as she muttered the startled question. 'What are you doing in my room?'

He didn't answer; he was staring at her fixedly, his

eyes narrowed. Nicole stared back and felt her body tense; still dazed from sleep, she hadn't recognised him for the first few seconds, he had changed so much. Eight years is a long time in anybody's life, and a good deal had happened to Frazer during those eight years; she saw the grim maturity in his harsh, unsmiling face, and confusion held her immobile, she wasn't able to think with any clarity.

'My God,' he said on a husky breath, 'how you've changed! I wouldn't have recognised you.' His eyes kept moving; over her hair, her features, the half concealed shape of her body under the sheet.

'I don't know who you are or why you've broken into my room, but you'd better get out now before I call the police,' Nicole said, forcing herself to concentrate on staying cool. He had taken her by surprise; which gave him an advantage she did not mean him to keep.

She saw the flicker of surprise in his face, the narrowing of the hard blue eyes, and while he hesitated she reached for the telephone beside the bed, one hand clutching the sheet around her.

'If you're not gone in ten seconds . . .' she began, picking up the receiver.

He took three steps and this time it was Nicole who was taken by surprise. His sinewy brown hand flashed down, clamped her wrist and forced the telephone back on the stand.

'Let go of me!' she exclaimed, hot colour sweeping up her face. 'I don't know who you are . . .'

'Like hell you don't!' he muttered, biting the words off with his teeth.

Nicole tugged at her tethered hand. The last thing she wanted to do was make a scene, attract attention to herself, and as she glared into his eyes she suddenly saw that he was aware of that, that the blue eyes were mocking her coldly, daring her to do anything about it.

'You wouldn't want me to scream,' she said, and one eyebrow rose, he half smiled but without humour.

'Wouldn't I?'

She trembled with rage. 'Get out of here, damn you!' Then her mind cleared and the confused feminine reactions to his unexpected appearance drained out of her. Her face smoothed out, her green eyes glowed, she was still for a moment as she pulled herself together to act. Slowly she relaxed backwards, smiling, pulling him downward towards her. She saw his face a second before she moved again. He was staring at her, every muscle tense. Then Nicole's free hand struck sideways, and Frazer Holt rolled before she could connect, swinging off the bed in one easy movement. He was on his feet when she looked up at him.

'Well, well, well,' he said very softly. 'Now where did you learn that? Is that a nice way for a lady to behave?'

'Get out of my room!' She was annoyed with herself for failing to take him by surprise, she was furious with him for the sardonic amusement in his stare.

'Not until you tell me what you're doing here, Nicole.'

She mimed surprise. 'Do I know you?' Eyes wide, she frowned. 'Have we met before?'

'Cut the comedy,' he advised her drily. 'You hadn't been on the island five minutes before I'd been told about the beautiful blonde English lady who'd sailed all the way from Athens alone and whose name was Nicole Lawton. Now it is possible that there are two Nicole

Lawtons in this world, but the likelihood of them both being blonde and both loving to sail is remote, wouldn't you say?'

She gave him a sweet smile when he paused to survey her. 'You're doing the talking. I never answer rhetorical questions.'

'You're going to answer some of my questions,' he promised.

'Make me,' Nicole mocked, sitting up, then wondering if perhaps that had been a mistake since her night-dress was very low cut and she found the flick of Frazer's blue eyes as he glanced over her extremely disturbing.

'Oh, I will,' he assured her. 'Starting with this one—what are you doing on Mykonos?'

'Having a holiday?' she suggested.

He smiled tightly, shaking his black head in a distinctly menacing way. 'Try again.'

'Sailing around the Greek islands for a holiday,' she said, and could well believe that Bevis's Greek detective had retreated hurriedly if he had met a welcome like this. Frazer wasn't even really trying yet, either. He was standing there at ease, an infuriating self-assurance in his manner, watching her coolly, his eyes hard, but she could imagine that if he chose he could become much nastier.

What was he thinking as he stared at her? Those blue eyes made her nervous, and that annoyed her even more. Not much made her nervous and she did not like feeling suddenly vulnerable, stripped of the armour she was accustomed to wearing.

'You've changed,' he said suddenly. 'I hardly know you.'

'You *don't* know me,' Nicole told him, and felt a bitter pleasure in saying it. Looking at his tanned face with icy contempt, she smiled, hoping he could read her thoughts.

If he did, he hid it behind the shrug he gave. 'Okay, have it your own way. You're here by chance, you're sailing around the Greek islands . . .'

'That's right,' she said.

'So sail away,' Frazer told her shortly. 'And tomorrow. You'll be sorry if I find you here again tomorrow night—next time I won't be so gentlemanly about it. I don't want you on this island.' He turned on his heel and walked to the door. As he opened it, Nicole flung at his back: 'How's Melanie?'

It checked him in mid-stride, he halted, looked back at her, the blue eyes deadly. 'Goodbye, Nicole,' he said, and the door slammed.

'And a Merry Christmas to you, too!' she shouted after him, then slid down the bed with a long sigh of slack relief at the removal of his nerve-racking presence, curving her arms above her head and linking her hands together. Did he really imagine his threat would drive her away? He could think again, she wasn't budging. She hadn't expected him to take the bait so fast, but the speed and force of his reaction had already told her a great deal. If she had ever wondered how much reliance to place on what Bevis had said about being warned off, Frazer had made sure she would stop wondering. Bevis hadn't imagined a thing, but then had she ever really thought he had? She would not be here if she hadn't intuitively believed what Bevis said.

Whether Bevis was crazy in believing that his sister had been murdered or not, one fact was very clear—

Melanie had been desperately unhappy with Frazer, he had treated her with cold selfishness. Nicole's old affection for Melanie had come flooding back at the news of her death, she regretted her anger now, she wished she had never vanished from Melanie's life. Melanie had been spoilt and wilful, but under that there had been something so lovable—a wild gaiety, a personal charm, that Nicole had always found irresistible whatever Melanie did, until the day Melanie went too far, and even then it had been Frazer she blamed, most of her bitter anger had been spent on him.

She meant to find out as much of the truth about Melanie's death as she could; she owed her that much. Bevis had got nowhere; his accusations had been too wild, too violent. Nicole wouldn't make that mistake. She was just going to talk to people, pick up every little clue she could. Melanie could have committed suicide, she could have drowned from sheer lack of will to live—Nicole didn't know how it had happened, but she meant to find out.

Frazer had already told her a great deal merely by bursting in here at night in a tearing rage. He wouldn't have done that if he had had nothing to hide. Her brows jerked together in a painful frown. What if Frazer *had* caused Melanie's death? What would she do if she uncovered real evidence against him?

For the first time she herself was emotionally involved in the situation she was busy investigating; instead of being a logical exercise she was coolly working out this was very personal. She had to face the fact that it was possible she would get hurt. She pushed the realisation away, shivering. She would deal with that some other time. In the meantime, she would let Frazer make all the running, waste his energy in attack while she smiled and held off. Keep him guessing, she thought, drifting into sleep.

CHAPTER THREE

WHEN she woke up the room was full of drifting sunlight and she heard voices outside in the street; the little town was waking up, too, she smelt coffee and the delicious fragrance of new-baked bread. She stretched, yawning, her body beautifully rested. Even Frazer Holt hadn't managed to stop her sleeping last night, nor did she remember dreaming. She must have slept far too deeply. Glancing at her watch, she saw it was almost eight o'clock. The air was cool, the building opposite left dark blue smudges of shadow on her walls and the sun hadn't yet fully arisen.

She rolled over towards the bedside table and picked up the phone to place a call to London. She had to let Sam know that she had arrived in Mykonos safely; he would worry about her if she didn't keep him informed.

There was a delay on the international lines, she was told; the operator would ring back when she managed to place the call.

Replacing the receiver, Nicole lay back with her arms crossed behind her head and her slim body relaxed while she considered what she should do that day. She was in no hurry—this was a holiday, after all, even if she did intend to do a little investigating on the side.

She would wander around the shops, take a look at Mykonos on foot at her leisure, then have a leisurely lunch at one of the waterside tavernas she had noticed as she sailed into harbour last night. From past experience of Greek towns she guessed that their food would be delicious; mostly seafood caught locally and always fresh and well cooked.

After that, she would casually saunter through the streets until she found Frazer Holt's house. She must discover where it was; it would help her to visualise Melanie's life here if she saw the house where she had pined for London. It must have been torture for her; Melanie had always been a city girl, she had never been drawn towards the countryside, that was why it had been Nicole who met Frazer Holt in the first place.

She had been sailing with Sam that summer. They had gone up north to explore the seas around the Hebrides in fine, calm weather which had lasted for weeks and looked like turning that summer into one of the summers people always remember. Sam was a good sailor; experienced but careful, he would never let Nicole take risks without thinking first, he taught her to calculate her chances before tackling anything.

At nineteen, Nicole had been daring; inclined to act suddenly without thinking of the consequences, and Sam had never let up on a chance to teach her the stupidity of being reckless. He had the sort of patience that is stubborn and doesn't wear out; he grimly went on repeating his message until Nicole finally got it. Looking back, she could see how deeply Sam had imprinted his seal on her character. People you know in early life have a much more powerful effect than anyone you meet later—you, yourself, are more plastic, more receptive to influences. It is later that you begin to harden and become impermeable.

Late one afternoon, just as the blue sky was deepening with twilight and the sun was beginning to colour the western horizon with flame and gold, they put into Mallaig; a large fishing port on the shores of North Morar on the West Coast with the mysterious darkening waters of Loch Morar behind it, but out of sight from the harbour, and across the Sound of Sleat in the distance the shimmering blueish hills of the island of Skye. The harbour was crammed with fishing boats and small yachts like their own; above the town reared heather-clad rocky hillsides whose dark green outline stretched starkly behind the white houses huddled at the water's edge. Only sheep as surefooted as mountain goats could graze on the windy, exposed slopes.

Nicole left Sam talking to some of the fishermen on the quayside and went to do some shopping; they had to restock before they sailed on again next morning to the islands. She bought bread and cheese and a variety of fruit; they ate simply on board, the less cooking there was to do the better, although Sam was quite ready to take his turn with the cooking and could turn out a very edible form of stew which he made by chucking every-thing available into one pot and leaving it to simmer for an hour or so; the flavours were often surprising but usually pleasant.

Nicole attracted the occasional glance from men who passed her; her long blonde hair was her chief attraction; she wore it normally in a single thick plait which hung down her back, swaying with her as she walked in a coltish, long-legged stride more like a boy's than a girl's. She was wearing very brief shorts and a cotton t-shirt, her smooth brown skin untouched by make-up, her green eyes very bright as she looked curiously around her at the weathered, whitewashed houses, whose sturdy structures bore witness to their need to withstand the winter onslaughts of sea winds.

She was so busy staring around her that she walked into someone without having noticed him. 'Sorry, I wasn't looking where I was going,' she stammered as the man steadied her, his hands on her shoulders. Her eyes had widened as she took in his tough good looks.

'No, you weren't, were you?' he had agreed mockingly, but he had smiled, too, and she had been flustered by the way his blue eyes gleamed down at her. 'Here to sail? Didn't I see you come in just now with your father—he is your father, I presume? I'm not putting my foot in it?'

'He's my uncle, but my parents are dead and in a way he's my father,' she had told him confusedly, and he had laughed. She had found his scrutiny disturbing; his eyes were too penetrating and there was keen intelligence in his face. At nineteen she was prickly about her looks; she wanted to be small and curvy and feminine, like Melanie. She despised her own looks; her breasts had barely developed, small and firm, they scarcely lifted her t-shirt, and her narrow hips and flat stomach gave her a boyish figure.

She had looked at her watch hurriedly to cover her confusion and said she must rush before the shops closed. 'Okay, see you later,' he had said calmly, and walked off, leaving her wondering if he had meant that, or it had merely been a polite phrase.

When she got back to the boat, however, she found him talking to Sam and drinking a mug of Sam's horrible black tea, with every appearance of relish. He had looked up and grinned at her and she had flushed with pleasure and surprise.

'Frazer tells me he ran into you,' Sam had said drily.

'Literally,' Frazer said with teasing amusement, and she had been angry because she was afraid he was laughing at her.

'He's cruising the islands, too,' Sam said, eyeing her curiously and with thoughtful speculation. 'Where do you head for next, Frazer?'

Frazer had answered and the two men had talked while Nicole put away her purchases.

'Why don't we have dinner in the town tonight? It may be the last chance any of us get, for a few days, of eating in comfortable surroundings?' Frazer had spoken to Sam, but he had gone on looking at Nicole and she had felt a strange happiness beginning inside her as she felt his eyes on her. She had never had a boy-friend, never met anyone like Frazer before, she knew nothing about men except what she had learnt from Sam and her own father. When Bevis had tried to kiss her the year before she had pushed him away in embarrassed impatience; boys of her own age did not interest her, and she knew *she* did not interest the men who usually interested *her*, she was far too young and far too gauche. Frazer was the first attractive man who had ever shown much interest in her.

'Would you like that, Nicole?' Sam had asked, and she had nodded, too breathless to speak.

It had been a marvellous evening. They had eaten in a crowded restaurant a short walk from the quayside; there was little choice on the menu, but the food itself was traditional Scots food, beautifully cooked and served, and perfect for hungry people who have spent a day on the sea with the wind and water to combat. They had started with broth, rich with fresh vegetables and barley in a lamb stock; then gone on to grilled salmon steaks—caught, they were assured, that morning not far away, and dressed with a delicate sauce, and followed that with pancakes served with blueberries.

It was very late when they walked back to the quay; Nicole had been heady with excitement. Sam went to bed right away, but she had sat on the deck talking in a low tone to Frazer, or rather listening to him as he talked; the conversation had ranged from world politics to books, from music to sailing, from travelling in foreign parts to the fascination of London.

Frazer had looked at his watch and made a face. 'Gone midnight! I must get some sleep and so must you, or you won't be much use to Sam tomorrow.' He had stood up and she had sat there looking up at him with vulnerable, dreaming eyes, unwilling to see him leave, unwilling to end the magic of the evening.

Frazer had contemplated her briefly, an odd wry look in his eyes, then he had bent and softly touched his lips against her mouth.

'See you,' he had said, and then he was gone, and she had sat on in the warm darkness listening to the surge of the sea and entranced by her thoughts.

In the morning when she went on deck he had gone and Sam was slightly irritable as he prepared to sail. Nicole had felt her spirits sink, she did not imagine she would ever see Frazer again, and suddenly all the pleasure with which she had been contemplating this holiday had evaporated.

She had been wrong; when they reached the harbour of Portree on Skye, Frazer met them on the quayside, his eyes amused as he watched Nicole's face flush and light up. He spent the evening with them again and next morning sailed off saying: 'See you in Stornoway.' Sam stood on the deck, staring at Nicole's averted profile, his expression troubled and uncertain.

'He's far too old for you, you know that,' he had murmured, and she had stared across the shimmering blue water without answering.

'It isn't just the eight years between you,' Sam had added. 'He's kicked around the world too much; these journalists do. That's a tough character, he'll only hurt you.'

When Nicole still ignored him Sam had shrugged and sighed. 'Well, I warned you,' he had said, and when they got to Stornoway on the island of Lewis two days later, after cruising slowly around the smaller uninhabited islands between Lewis and Skye, his smile had not betrayed his doubts as he saw Frazer walking towards them, a hand lifted in greeting. Sam liked Frazer; Nicole had never thought otherwise, she knew Sam too well. If he didn't like someone he made it very clear, to her, at least.

It was at Stornoway that Nicole discovered how tough Frazer could be, how dangerous he was in a temper. They were all three walking back from the town centre late that night when Nicole stopped to stroke a black cat which ran across their path. The two men walked on, talking, and just as she was going to catch them up someone came up behind her and grabbed her by the waist. It was a total stranger, Nicole only had time to see his face briefly before he kissed her, his breath smelling of whisky and making her shudder. She struggled violently, unable to scream because his mouth silenced her. Then Frazer must have turned and seen what was going on, because the next minute the drunk was reeling back from her and Frazer was hitting him. Nicole shrank back, a hand to her bruised mouth. Sam pulled Frazer off the man who, by then, was bleeding copiously. 'That's enough, for God's sake, man!' Sam exclaimed, and Nicole saw Frazer's hard face clenched in a rage which altered his whole expression. His chest was heaving, his breathing audible. It was five minutes before he calmed down enough to ask Nicole tersely: 'Are you okay?'

He, himself, had rarely kissed her, although over the next few weeks they were often together. It became something of a game with them for Frazer to beat them to a port; he grinned in triumph as they sailed in an hour or two after him. Sam tried getting up earlier, but Frazer's boat was faster and sleeker; he always won their unofficial little race. He had a ciné camera with him and had taken film of them and of the incredible scenery he saw during the voyage. 'You must come to dinner and show us the film when it has been developed,' Sam said on the last night before they turned back to England, and Nicole had held her breath waiting for Frazer to answer. He had given her a smile, his eyes warm. 'That's a date,' he had said, and she had known he was saying it to her, not Sam, and been so happy she hadn't known how to hide it. By then she had been deeply in love with him; with all the aching intensity of first love which is uncertain of itself and has not yet felt a response.

The telephone rang, breaking into her thoughts, and she was almost startled to find herself in the Hotel Delos, lying on the bed with closed eyes and a mind totally absorbed in memories of the past.

Rolling over, she snatched up the receiver and heard the deep-sea rustling and booming of the international line. A moment later Sam yelled: 'That you? Everything okay?'

'I'm on Mykonos now, I had a terrific time sailing here from Athens, the weather's perfect, plenty of wind but the sea quite calm.' She paused and Sam made a grumbling noise.

'Wish I was with you. How long are you staying on Mykonos?'

'A few days,' she evaded, not wanting to tell him the truth. 'How's work?'

'Lousy, my desk's piled so high I can't see over the top of all the paper.' He talked about several cases in which Nicole had been involved, asking her questions she answered as briefly as possible, her face wry. It all seemed so far away, she couldn't get excited about work at the moment.

'This call's costing the earth,' said Sam. 'I hope you aren't charging it to the firm.'

'Cheapskate,' she teased, laughing. 'I'll keep in touch and let you know when I'll be back. Look after yourself and don't work too hard.'

'Get back here in one piece, I need you,' Sam said gruffly, and she blew him a kiss before she hung up.

Sliding off the bed, she chose the clothes she meant to wear that day and laid them ready on the bed. As she passed the small dressing-table mirror she saw herself and felt the jolt of surprise she always got when she caught sight of her own reflection; she had changed so much. Frazer had been right about that—she had changed drastically, and the change had begun because of him.

She hadn't meant to tell Melanie about Frazer; during the journey back to London she had thought about it and decided to keep him a secret, the first real secret she had ever kept from Melanie, but she was too excited. She forgot to be cautious, she forgot why she did not want Melanie to know about him, she was reckless with pride and joy and it all poured out. Melanie had listened open-mouthed; her first disbelief melting as she watched Nicole's glowing face.

'He's got to be married,' she had said, pricking Nicole's balloon, because that had never occurred to her, but once she thought about it she saw that Frazer was far too attractive to be unmarried.

'Did he make love to you?' Melanie had asked then, and Nicole had been torn between telling the truth and allowing Melanie to think he had; she had settled in the end for a shrug and silence.

'Did he? Or was Sam playing watchdog as usual?' Melanie had insisted. 'You let Sam spoil your fun too much, how can you enjoy yourself if he's always around?' She had laughed wickedly. 'Bevis doesn't interfere with my fun; he knows what would happen if he tried.' Then she had murmured: 'He's a Fleet Street journalist, did you say? Is he famous?' Later she had asked: 'When are you seeing him? Or didn't he suggest meeting again?' and Nicole had stupidly told her about the film Frazer had made of their trip and that when it was ready he would come round and show it to them.

Melanie hadn't commented to her, but a few days later she had said to Sam: 'I'm dying to see this film of your holiday in the Hebrides; don't forget to tell me when I can come round and see it.'

Sam had grunted without promising anything of the kind; he was fond of Melanie the way he might be amused by a playful kitten, briefly, before tiring of it. As long as he did not see too much of her she seemed to make him laugh; but to Nicole he had once said impatiently: 'That girl's spoilt and set on getting her own way; far too much money too young, I suppose.' Melanie's father had been generous with money for as long as Nicole could remember him, but he had never taken any real interest in either of his children, apart from making sure that they had everything material that they could want. It had been Bevis who had been Melanie's guiding influence when she was small and Bevis had adored and petted her; he had always given her everything she wanted, too.

'She's highly strung,' Nicole had defended.

'Nonsense,' Sam had muttered. 'That's just an excuse; she never thinks of anyone but herself.'

'That isn't fair! You know she loves Bevis dearly.'

'She loves her brother because he never says no to her; it's easy to love someone who hands you everything on a plate.'

'She's fond of me,' Nicole had said, her mouth warm with affection, and Sam had stared at her, his brows beetling.

'The same answer applies,' he had said, and Nicole had had to think about that before she understood what he meant, and then she had been hurt because Sam had been implying that Melanie only loved her because she loved Melanie. Nicole was not someone who gave her affection lightly; the only two people in the world she had ever loved since her parents died had been Melanie and Sam. Sam was solid and real and essential to her; she trusted him absolutely and usually accepted everything he said as gospel. But not when he criticised Melanie— Nicole had memories of Melanie that Sam did not have;

she knew her far better. She had first met her when they were both nervous new girls at their school; Melanie had been very small and enchantingly pretty even in school uniform, its formal look merely emphasised her vivid features and delicate, appealing smile. Nicole had been all arms and legs and stammering shyness; the other girls had either ignored her or made fun of her. That had made Melanie angry, she had glared at them and put an arm around Nicole when she was being teased, and soon Nicole was left alone, because everyone adored Melanie and nobody wanted to offend her. She rapidly became one of the most popular girls in the school and she continued to prefer Nicole's company, which surprised and delighted Nicole.

Melanie was impulsive, generous, high-spirited, fun; kind-hearted if anyone was unhappy and often quite silly; giggling when the games mistress slipped on an icy patch in the playground and sprawled at her feet, playing practical jokes on teachers which would have got anyone else into serious trouble. Nicole couldn't forget those years of whispering to each other in class, lending each other tennis racquets or books, listening to the latest pop music after school while they did their homework together.

Nicole had known her so well, yet she hadn't guessed that from the minute she first heard about Frazer, Melanie had been fascinated by all she was told about him. Maybe she had made up her mind there and then to make a play for him—whatever her original intentions, from the minute she actually saw Frazer the end was never in any real doubt.

It had been six weeks later; autumn was deepening the colour of the leaves and a crisp dry chill hovered in the air. Frazer rang up to say he had the film and by chance Melanie had been there when Sam got the call; she had begged for an invitation to dinner that night. When Frazer arrived he had kissed Nicole, and with Melanie watching she had deliberately put her arms round his neck for a second as she kissed him back. At the time she hadn't been trying to show Melanie that he was her property; she had simply wanted Melanie to be convinced that Frazer was more than just an acquaintance; In a sense she had been showing off, and she had paid for that later, because her brief gesture had been an attempted claim on him and her later humiliation had been all the more intense.

Frazer had looked at Melanie with surprise, his eyes widening at her beauty. They had shaken hands and Melanie had smiled brilliantly, but that evening Frazer had not seemed totally bowled over. He had talked to Nicole all through dinner; asking her how her work was going, teasing her about the fact that she had put up her long hair that evening, coiled it round into a sleek chignon. He had talked about his own job; made private jokes, reminding her of things that had happened during the holiday in Scotland.

Afterwards had shown the film, then Melanie had left. Frazer had stayed until one in the morning, talking to Nicole. She had been stupid with happiness, she hadn't been able to get to sleep that night. Frazer had invited her to see a play in the West End the following week. She had gone and did not remember one single thing about the play they saw; all she knew was that she was with Frazer. He had driven her home and in the car outside the flat she had let him kiss her properly for the first time; he had gently undone her long hair and let it spill over her shoulders, running his fingers through it. Nicole had closed her eyes and run her arms round his neck, breathless with pleasure and excitement, and Frazer had slipped his hand inside her dress and touched her breast; nobody had ever touched her so intimately before, she had felt herself go dizzy and had trembled violently.

'Am I frightening you?' Frazer had asked uncertainly, feeling the tremor running through her and she had shaken her head and whispered: 'No, no . . .' She had ached for him to caress her, to make love to her for hours, but he had drawn back and done up her dress and said it was getting late, he had better go. He had asked her to come out again the following weekend and she had been walking on air. Melanie had stared at her next day and said: 'It's a mistake to let a man see you're crazy about him.' Nicole had flushed, hotly embarrassed.

'He'll only take you for granted,' Melanie had added.

'Frazer's different,' Nicole had insisted, believing it. She was going out with Melanie that evening; Bevis was driving them across London to some party given by friends of Melanie's and Nicole wished she had not said she would go, but Melanie would only be aggrieved if she backed out, so she sighed and got up.

'I'll go and get ready, I won't be ten minutes.'

While she was changing her dress she heard the telephone ring and ran downstairs a moment later, on tenterhooks in case it was Frazer, but Melanie told her it had been Bevis ringing to check if they would be ready in a quarter of an hour for him to pick them up; she was still talking to her brother, she held out the phone to Nicole and said: 'Tell him he's a pest.'

Nicole had laughed and said into the receiver: 'You're

a pest!' then handed it back to Melanie, before walking out to finish doing her make-up.

When Bevis arrived he made a growling noise at her: 'So I'm a pest, am I?' He was in an odd humour that evening, she remembered; almost wild, reckless with high spirits which were on the edge of being neurotic. Even at that age she had sometimes wondered if Bevis was on drugs; his moods so volatile, you never knew how you would find him, the unpredictability was more than adolescent temperament.

The party had been as dull as she had feared, although both Bevis and Melanie had had a good time, if their laughter was anything to go by. All she had been thinking of, though, was Frazer, she was aching to see him again, she could not wait for the following Saturday.

She had been ready hours before he was due to pick her up. She sat watching the clock, waiting; her happiness and excitement slowly leaked away as she saw the hours tick past without Frazer arriving. She rang his flat and he did not answer. She made excuses for him to herself; perhaps he had suddenly been sent away on a story, and had forgotten their date in his hurry or maybe he had had an accident or was taken ill. At midnight she went to bed while Sam watched her with heavy brows, having tactfully said nothing. Alone, she broke down and cried, but next day she started waiting for Frazer to ring and explain, apologise, make another date. He never rang again, but it was a week before she admitted to herself that Frazer had simply stood her up.

Melanie had gone away around that time; to Paris, to visit another old school friend. Her absence made it easier for Nicole; she didn't have to answer any awkward questions, and by the time Melanie reappeared Nicole was over the worst, she had begun to forget Frazer with the ferocity of someone determined to amputate some part of themselves which hurts badly. Melanie was lit up when she came back; she refused to talk about it, but she hinted that she was in love, and her odd secrecy made Nicole laugh. She let Melanie keep her secret, however, without pressing to be told all about the new boy-friend; Nicole had learnt the necessity of keeping some things to yourself.

When Melanie came to see her a few months later and said: 'I'm getting married to Frazer,' Nicole had just stood there going white and unable to ask any questions.

Melanie had looked away, flushed and uneasy. 'I know I should have told you I was seeing him, but I didn't want to upset you, I didn't know how you'd feel about it and it's months since you even mentioned his name, so you obviously weren't that keen on him, were you? Oh, Nicole, I'm crazy about him, he's the most . . .'

'How long has it been going on?' Nicole had asked, breaking into the hastily chattered sentences, and her voice had been stiff and chill, each word broken off like a razor-sharp splinter of ice.

'I met him in Paris while I was visiting Emma; he was there on a story.' Melanie had looked anywhere but at Nicole; she was smiling too much and the smiles did not reach her eyes.

Unbelievably Melanie had said: 'Will you be my bridesmaid?' and Nicole had said tersely: 'No.'

When Melanie left she paused and almost whispered: 'Won't you wish me good luck?' and Nicole had tried to say: 'I hope you'll both be happy,' but she couldn't get the words out, she would not have meant them, at that precise moment she hoped they would both be very unhappy—and maybe she had ill-wished them, because if what Bevis said was true, they had not been happy, the marriage had not worked.

Afterwards she had been angry with herself for letting Melanie see the damage Frazer had done her, for allowing her pride to slip so far that she couldn't pretend she didn't care. She had woken up in the night for a long time, hot and sick with shame, hating both of them and hating herself for having betrayed her sense of humiliation to Melanie. That had been the formative incident of her life: after that she had concentrated with bitter intensity on toughening herself both mentally and physically. No one, ever again, was going to hurt her.

But, however angry with Melanie she had been once, she had forgiven her now. The Melanie she forgave was not the girl who married Frazer—Nicole forgave and mourned the Melanie of her childhood; the girl who had put an arm round her when other girls made fun of her and shouted at them to leave Nicole alone, the girl who had giggled over silly jokes with her and whispered secrets as they walked to school.

That Melanie, she recognised, had been dead for her for a long time, but it was not until now that Nicole could openly face the fact and allow herself to feel grief.

CHAPTER FOUR

WHEN she had had a shower and dressed in pale blue pants and a sleeveless white shirt she went downstairs in search of breakfast and found Irena Vourlamis at the reception desk, her head bent over a slip of paper.

'Good morning,' said Nicole, and Irena looked up, but there was no answering smile in her eyes, she looked nervous and uneasy.

'Good morning. I have laid breakfast for you in the dining-room; I will make some fresh coffee now and bring it to you.' She stepped back and opened a door, and with a nod Nicole walked into the small room beyond, wondering if Irena's sudden coolness arose because of Frazer Holt. Had he talked to Irena last night? Well, he must have done, she thought; frowning. How else would he have known her room number? In fact, he must have had a pass key or he couldn't have got into her room in the first place. What had he said to Irena to explain why he wanted a key?

A table had been laid with a cup and saucer, a plate and cutlery, and, in the centre, a basket of rolls and some tiny little cakes which looked like fairy cakes. Nicole sat down and split one of the rolls, spread it thinly with butter and some of the thick dark cherry jam in a glass dish. She had just taken a bite of the roll when Irena entered the room with a large pot of coffee in one hand and an English newspaper in the other.

'Three days old, I am afraid, but I thought you might

like something to read,' she explained politely as she placed them both on the table.

'Thank you,' Nicole murmured.

'If you wanted milk . . .'

'I prefer my coffee black.' Nicole smiled at her, pouring herself some of the strong coffee. Irena hovered and after a moment Nicole looked up enquiringly, her brows lifting. The other woman was flushed and seemed unhappy about something.

'I will have your bill ready after breakfast,' Irena said, and Nicole put down the cup she had been about to lift to her mouth.

'I'm not leaving today; I've booked for two weeks.'

'I'm sorry, I'm afraid I have to close up the hotel, I must ask you to leave.' Irena looked restlessly away and then hurried out of the room. Nicole stared after her, frowning. What on earth could Frazer have said to her to persuade her to throw Nicole out? Nicole finished her meal without hurrying, but she was irritated; she liked Irena and she found the hotel very comfortable, she did not want to have to move.

When she emerged into the lobby Irena was standing at the desk. She pushed a bill across the polished wood. Nicole stared at her and made no move to take it.

'I am going to see Frazer Holt this morning, I will be back later,' she said, and turned on her heel. Behind her she felt Irena take a startled breath, move as if to catch her arm, then the other woman let her arm drop and Nicole walked out of the hotel into the sharp sunlight which was beginning to pattern the street in black and white; blindingly bright on one side and thick shadow on the other.

There were no pavements here; the narrow alleys ran

between houses and shops, crisscrossing each other and curling round upon themselves in loops in that haphazard way as though a drunkard had laid out the streets as he reeled home after an evening spent in the taverna. The houses had the same unplanned air: some of them mere concrete boxes, glaringly white in the sun, some of them elaborately designed yet strangely timeless with narrow wooden balconies on the upper floors, painted wooden columns supporting them below and wooden shutters closed across the windows, to exclude the searing heat of the sun. They reminded Nicole of the houses she had seen in the Roman ruins of Herculaneum; the design was often almost identical although centuries lay between. Some of the houses seemed to have a Turkish influence, with stark white arches of stone leading into an inner courtyard of shade and flowers.

Nicole knew the name of Frazer Holt's house and Mykonos was so small, she was sure she would find it quickly. She walked slowly, staring through tiny arched doorways hung with drifting white wool shawls made locally by tanned, weatherbeaten old women in black whom she saw sitting in the shade spinning. Some of the shops sold leather goods or brass ornaments; some sold exotic gauzy dresses or shirts, others gaily decorated local pottery. Between the shops lay the houses, and she stared at each one looking for the name of it. It was only after half an hour that she realised she was lost; it seemed so unbelievable, she had walked round and round inside the convoluted streets like an ant in a maze, and now she was passing the same houses, the same shops, and she hadn't yet set eyes on Frazer's house.

The sun had risen higher, the air was hot and she was tired, and thirsty. She walked down to the harbour front and sat down at a pavement café to drink freshly squeezed citrus juice; a mixture of orange and lemon sweetened with sugar and very refreshing. A pelican stood in the shadow of a boat, clacking its great beak as it watched the sea slapping on to the narrow beach.

When she paid the young man who had brought her the drink she asked him how to find Frazer's house. He stared at her, black eyes unwinking, then without a word pointed vaguely before disappearing back into the café.

Nicole got up and almost fell over the outstretched feet of a man at the next table. 'Sorry,' he said, and she looked at him sharply; surprised to hear an English voice. He gave her a polite smile. 'Are you on holiday here?'

'Yes, you too?'

'I'm living here,' he said, and she felt a dart of interest. That could be very useful; he might have picked up the sort of gossip she needed to hear.

'What a lovely place to live—I don't think I've seen anywhere like it, even in Greece.'

'Pure cubist,' he agreed with a nod. 'A perfect place for a painter—the light is incredible, of course, especially in the spring. It has its drawbacks—in winter the winds nearly take your head off.'

'It's very exposed,' she murmured, looking past him at the crowded streets of the small town. 'Have you been here long?'

'A few months.' He gestured to the empty chairs at his table. 'Won't you join me? Can I get you another drink?'

'Thank you, I'd like a coffee,' said Nicole, sitting down opposite him.

'Pavlo!' he shouted, and the young waiter appeared,

his face expressionless as he glanced from one to the other of them. 'Coffee, *parakalo*.'

The waiter disappeared without so much as a nod. Nicole smiled at the man facing her. 'I'm Nicole Lawton.'

'Hallo,' he said again. 'I'm William Oldfield, and I hate being called Bill or Will. I'm William.' He had a rather precise way of speaking; slightly fussy.

She smiled again. 'Did you say you were a painter?'

He hesitated, running a hand over his thick, curly brown hair; he wore it very long, almost down to the collar of his short-sleeved blue shirt.

'Not exactly.' He seemed uncertain how to answer, and she lifted her brows.

'Oh?' Was he an amateur? she wondered. How did he earn a living here on Mykonos? Why was he looking embarrassed?

'I went to art school and I do paint,' he explained. 'But I actually earn my daily bread by writing travel books. I'm doing a series for an American publisher; illustrated guides to Greek islands. I write the text and provide the photographs and some pen and ink sketches.'

'Do they sell well?'

He shrugged. 'I earn enough to live on. I sell some of my paintings to tourists, too, I do okay. I enjoy the work.'

'That's a very good reason for doing anything,' she agreed, and he looked at her hard, as though suspecting she was making fun of him, then smiled. He was a tall, thin man, around thirty, she suspected; his eyes a very pale grey, their lack of colour accentuated by his deeply tanned skin. He was wearing blue jeans which had been so well washed that they were fading to a neutral shade, his feet were brown and pushed into plastic flip-flops of the kind you saw hanging up in many of the shops here.

'The great thing about this job is that I can learn while I earn,' he told her, relaxing with a grin. 'I'm trying to study Greek art.'

'How long does it take to write one of these books?'

'Not long; the text is easy, they're very short books. I chose Mykonos as my base because it's so close to Athens. I've got my own boat, you see—I can pretty well come and go as I choose when the weather's good.'

'Did anybody famous ever live on Mykonos?' she asked casually as the waiter came out with her coffee. He put it in front of her, eyeing her with a wooden expression, and then vanished again.

'Oh, sure,' said William Oldfield, sipping his own drink; a long glass of mineral water. 'Mind you, Mykonos is more or less famous for not having any history; no great heroes or kings, no battles or tragedies. What you see now is what everyone has seen for centuries.' He gestured. 'Primitive, simple houses—little boxes, in fact. In a sense Mykonos was modern before the rest of Greece where they're busy building little boxes everywhere now.'

'Not just in Greece—we have them in England, too.'

'Too true.' He eyed her thoughtfully. 'What do you do, Nicole?'

'I'm in insurance,' she said, as she always did; people stared if you told them you were a private detective, their ideas were all based on Hollywood films about sharp-eyed men with guns. Nicole mainly earned her income from detecting insurance frauds for the big companies; it was largely paperwork, but when she did have to do some fieldwork it very rarely proved dangerous, merely time-consuming and often boring, requiring hours and hours of patient surveillance of a suspect.

William looked sympathetic. 'Pays well, I suppose,' he said.

Nicole smiled. 'Very well. Are there many painters and writers living here now?'

'Oh, a few. There's a poet living in one of the tavernas; crazy guy, Greek; he doesn't come out until it's dark and then he sits in the taverna drinking all night.'

'No English writers?' She tried to sound casual; William Oldfield might know Frazer, he might be talking to her deliberately to find out what she knew. She watched him through lowered lashes while she drank her coffee; it was strong and bitter, without sugar.

William fingered his glass, staring at it, then he looked up and gave her a wry smile. 'I know who you're getting at—yes, Frazer Holt lives here; everybody will tell you that. His latest film grossed millions in the States, they say. The guy is stinking rich.' His tone was acid and Nicole met his eyes curiously, half smiling.

'You don't like him?' Well, that's a relief, she thought.

'I don't like him,' William agreed flatly. 'I can't say I know him very well, because he's made sure I don't. When I first arrived I sat at a table with him and the Greek who owns the house I'm renting. Frazer Holt shook hands, said about three words to me and then ignored me for the rest of the evening. He's gone on ignoring me ever since.'

Nicole wondered why: William seemed pleasant enough, why had Frazer cut him dead like that?

'He's an arrogant bastard,' William told her. 'The people here seem to like him; he speaks fluent Greek, they all talk to him and he's friendly enough with them. Maybe he just doesn't like my face.' He laughed, but he didn't look very amused.

Nicole pushed her cup away. Lightly she murmured: 'Perhaps he was cut up over his wife's death; didn't she drown on Mykonos?'

'That was a few years back,' William said. 'And it was on Delos, so I heard; she shouldn't even have been on Delos, you aren't allowed to spend the night there; it's a restricted site, the whole island's a protected area, tourists are supposed to go round the sites with a guide. Nobody lives there but the site workers. Otherwise it's deserted. Heaven knows what Holt's wife was doing there at night.'

Nicole frowned. 'How do they know she was there if she drowned? Was her boat found?' Melanie had hated sailing; had she learnt to love it here in Greece? Had she sailed over to Delos alone to escape from Frazer? Or had she meant to die?

'One of the site workers found her clothes and a sleeping bag and a few other things down on the beach. There was no sign of her and only a few days later her body was washed up.' William raked back his hair, grimacing. 'And that's all I know, because as soon as I asked any questions everyone here clammed up. They're like that; clannish and secretive. If you don't seem interested they'll tell you endless stories about themselves and their families, but start asking questions and they shut up fast.' He stared at Nicole with a thoughtful expression. 'You're in insurance, you said. Would I be way off course if I guessed that you're here to check up on her death? Did Holt have a fat policy out on her?'

Nicole smiled. 'We didn't insure her, if he did, and I doubt if he needs any money. He's very successful, isn't he?'

'Successful and bloody rude,' said William, and she wondered if he was aggrieved because Frazer hadn't been more friendly to a fellow writer, especially one who was not as successful as himself, or if he was simply jealous of Frazer's popularity?

'Does he live in one of the modern villas up on the hill?' Nicole was still trying to sound casual, but she sensed that William had become suspicious of her constant questions, even though she had denied that she was investigating Melanie's death.

'No, he has an old house in the town; if you're thinking of calling on him my advice is don't, he isn't friendly.' William had turned sulky now, his mouth was curved downwards. 'Take the next turning, then turn left and bear to your right; his house has a mulberry tree in the courtyard and it has a pair of gates with a lion sitting on each side. It's painted white but the shutters are blue.'

Nicole stood up, and he stared downwards, his shoulders hunched. 'Thanks for the coffee, see you around again,' she said, and he flapped an irritated hand.

'Give my regards to Frazer Holt.' It was a petulant comment and she ignored it, walking away without looking back. She followed his directions, hoping that this time she would find her way; all the streets looked the same, meandering in and out and seeming to have no direction, although whenever she looked to her right she saw the blue sea sparkling between white walls.

Suddenly she saw a house with blue shutters and stopped outside the high gates. Over the top of the white wall she saw dark green leaves moving and stirring in a breeze, and on the low parapet on a columned balcony on the top floor she saw rows of red earthenware pots full of pink geraniums. She was just about to ring the bell when Frazer appeared on the balcony and stared down at her, his darkly tanned face set in hostility. He leaned on the parapet, his fingers gripping the edge; Nicole watched coolly and thought, as she had thought last night, how much he had altered; how hard and remote his face had become. His thick black hair showed a faint streak of silver in the strong sunlight; he must be in his late thirties by now. He was as lean and vital as he had been when she first met him, the changes had not been in his body, they had occurred in his mind and they were revealed in his face; in the icy inimical blue eyes, in the tough mouth and aggressive line of the jaw.

What was he thinking as he watched her? She wouldn't guess from his face; it told her that his mood was not welcoming, but it did not tell her much apart from that.

Still staring back at him, she pressed the bell. Frazer disappeared from the balcony and Nicole pressed the bell again, keeping her thumb on it. She wondered if he was going to let her go on ringing for ever; if he meant to ignore her altogether. She pushed at the gates, but they did not move; locked, no doubt. She glanced up at the walls; eight foot high, she reckoned, simple enough to climb over if you had help, but she wouldn't put it past Frazer to have her arrested for trespass if she did manage to get over the wall.

A moment later she heard a grating sound, the key turned and then the gate opened. Frazer leaned on it negligently; his long, lean body propped up by one hand.

He was wearing white pants and a thin black shirt which clung to his deep chest.

Nicole looked at him drily. 'What took you so long?'

'Why are you still here?' he asked in turn, without answering her deliberate mockery.

'I'm renewing an old acquaintance,' she said ambiguously, and saw a curious flicker in the blue eyes, as though he was smiling; then it was erased and his face went cold again.

'If you mean me, I'm very busy finishing my latest book, I'm afraid. I haven't got time to talk. Why don't you just get on your boat and make for somewhere more lively? Try Corfu—they have a lot to offer.'

'I'm staying here,' she said lightly, and with a frown Frazer stepped back. He began to shut the gate. Nicole crashed into it, sending him staggering backwards in surprise. She was inside the gate now, but she felt Frazer leap towards her, making a snarling sound.

Every nerve in her body prickled with anticipation, she swung to face him and he grabbed at her, his hands fastening on her shoulders.

'I'm not talking to you, Nicole,' he grated harshly, shaking her.

She twisted sideways and jerked her left arm with as much force as she could into his midriff. He gave a grunt and let go of her, astonishment in his face, then suddenly came back at her, his lip curling back from his white teeth.

Nicole swivelled, her hand clamping down on his fore-arm, one foot hooking around his ankle. A second later Frazer flew backwards and landed with a thud on the courtyard floor. He lay there, winded, for a moment, breathing thickly.

Nicole watched as he slowly sat up, rubbing the back of his head. 'My God, you little bitch,' he said without any sign of rage now. 'I'll be damned! Is this what you've been learning since I last saw you? I'd heard that London wasn't the safe city it used to be, but I hadn't realised that Englishwomen were turning into Amazons!'

'It's wise to be able to protect yourself,' said Nicole, feeling a stab of triumph, and he watched the little smile curving her mouth, his expression wry.

'You enjoyed that,' he accused.

'You'd better believe it,' she said, and openly laughed. 'Your face was a picture!'

'Hell, you took me by surprise.' He ran an exploratory hand over himself. 'I'm lucky not to have broken a few bones.' He held out the hand. 'Help me up.'

Her green eyes derided him. 'You have to be kidding! I take your hand and the next thing I know I'm flying over your head! If that stunt's been pulled on me once it's been pulled a dozen times. No, I'm sure you can get up on your own.'

She sauntered away, and glanced through the white archway into the courtyard beyond. Small and streaked with shadow, it contained white wooden seats and stone troughs of flowers; she didn't recognise the vivid blue petals which fluttered slightly in the breeze. A black cat lay curled up in the sun, sleeping lightly, nose on paws. Nicole walked through the archway towards it, smiling, but conscious of Frazer getting to his feet and coming behind her. He walked softly, like a cat, she barely heard him breathing and she was aware of every move he made even though she wasn't looking in his direction.

Without looking round at him she said coolly: 'Up to you if you want to try your luck again, of course—but take my advice. Don't. Next time I might hurt you.' She squatted down beside the cat and stroked it gently; it opened one eye to give her an appraising, slitted stare, then began to purr, the vibrations shaking its small body.

'Are you married?' Frazer asked, and that time he did surprise her; she turned her head to look at him, her eyes wide, and a tautness around her mouth.

'No.' The answer was given through almost closed lips.

'Someone had a lucky escape,' Frazer commented, but his stare stayed on her as though trying to read the reasons for her clipped reply. To her fury she felt a slight flush creep into her face; she didn't like what he had just said, from anyone else she would have laughed at it, but from Frazer Holt it was humiliating.

'Do you want some coffee?' he asked, glancing at his watch.

'Thank you.' Nicole stood up and the little cat stretched, sharp claws suddenly visible among the black fur. Nicole smiled as she watched it; she loved cats. Frazer was staring at it, too; an odd frown on his face.

'She reminds me of you,' he said drily. 'Silky and graceful and potentially deadly.'

Nicole's head shot round to focus a stare on him, he was already walking away across the courtyard to a door in the white wall on the left. The courtyard was paved with stone, his footsteps rang and bounced off the walls. There was no sign of anyone else here; the silence had a slumbrous, languid heaviness compounded of heat and dust and the scent of flowers held in between the four walls of the house which ran around the yard. When a bell began to clang somewhere she jumped in surprise;

other bells joined in and as Frazer opened the door he looked back at her.

'Mykonos is full of churches; over three hundred at the last count. One of them is always ringing a bell.'

'That must drive you crazy when you're trying to write,' Nicole commented, joining him.

'No, you get used to it—I hardly notice the bells now.' He walked into the shadowy house and she followed him along a whitewashed corridor hung with drawings and paintings, into a low-ceilinged room of rectangular shape. It was lined with books from floor to ceiling on all four sides. The floor was of pale pink marble; a few Turkish rugs were scattered on it. Nicole noticed a wide desk on which stood a typewriter and piles of books and manuscripts, but Frazer was turning to the right, so she quickened her steps to keep up with him. He opened another door and she saw beyond it a modern kitchen with polished wood cabinets and chrome fittings.

Frazer gestured to the table under a low-silled window looking out into the courtyard.

'I'll get the coffee,' he said, moving to the hob.

Nicole sat down and watched his wide shoulders, the long tapering line of his back. She felt strangely reluctant to start asking him the questions she had come here to ask; there were so many other questions she suddenly wanted to ask him. Eight years is a long time, she thought, and then to her shocked surprise heard Frazer saying it, speaking her own thoughts aloud.

'Eight years is a long time.' He paused as he pushed the percolator on to the hob. 'What have you been doing all this time, apart from learning how to chuck men over your shoulder? What is it, anyway? Judo?'

'I'm a black belt,' she said, and he looked round at her, his lips pursed in a silent whistle.

'Remind me not to make you angry!'

'I will,' said Nicole with dry irony, and a grimness came into his eyes.

'What the hell are you doing here, Nicole? And don't give me any fairy stories about being on holiday, because I don't buy it. You aren't here by accident. You knew I lived here, you came deliberately—why?'

'Melanie's buried here, isn't she?'

'Melanie's dead! Forget her and go back to England. What good do you think you'll do coming here? Why rake up the past after all this time?'

'I seem to remember you once told me that your motive for being a reporter was a passion for uncovering the truth. When did you change?' There was contempt in her gaze and Frazer saw it; his lip curled back from his teeth as though he was struggling with black rage.

'And what's your motive, Nicole? You haven't seen Melanie for years, why have you come here now?'

She was silent because she wasn't sure herself. She had thought her only feelings for him were scorn and dislike, but what she felt was more complex than that. She wondered suddenly if she was confusing what he had done to her with what she suspected he had done to Melanie, without being quite sure exactly what he had done to either of them. Frazer was ambivalent, puzzling—what sort of man was he? The torment of uncertainty had begun to grow inside her from the minute she first saw him again in the street outside the hotel. She had felt a dart of panic, a tremor of alarm—and hadn't she known then how dangerous it could be for her to see him again?

'Did Bevis send you?' Frazer asked abruptly when she didn't speak, and she pulled herself together.

'He doesn't even know I *am* here. I lost touch with Bevis years ago.'

Frazer stared at her, his brows jerking together, as though he didn't believe her.

'Then how did you know Melanie was dead?' he shot at her, and she shrugged casually.

'I have plenty of contacts in the press, I need them all the time in our business.'

Distracted by that, he asked: 'You still work for Sam? But of course you must, or you wouldn't be bothering with judo. I thought he specialised in discreet insurance investigation? That isn't dangerous work, surely?'

'Depends on the suspect,' she admitted. 'One guy who'd made a fraudulent claim worth nearly a hundred thousand paid some thugs to waylay me one dark night. I might have been killed; as it was I ended up in hospital with broken ribs and a broken arm. I don't like carrying guns; it's dangerous. Judo was fun and made me feel much safer.'

'You're an extraordinary creature,' Frazer said with a sort of angry force which yet was not precisely hostile, and she smiled at him.

'Thank you.' She supposed that that was a compliment.

'But you must stop asking questions about Melanie,' he said in a very different voice. 'Do you hear me, Nicole? I can't force you to leave Mykonos, if you're determined to stay, but I warn you—forget about Melanie, for your own sake.'

CHAPTER FIVE

'AND if I don't?' she asked contemptuously. 'What happens then? Will I wash up on a Greek beach one fine morning?' Her slanting green eyes mocked him and his mouth parted on a silent snarl; she thought for a moment he was going to hit her and tensed, waiting for a movement from him which never came.

'You'd better go,' he said, his lips barely moving but showing her the edge of straight white teeth clenched together.

'I haven't had my coffee; it's ready, by the sound of it.' It was audibly more than ready; hitting the top of the glass dome of the percolator in noisy agitation. Frazer swung round and snatched it off the hob. He got two stone-coloured pottery mugs out of a cupboard and poured the coffee, handing one mug to her as though he wanted to hurl it into her face.

'Thank you,' Nicole said with as dazzling a smile as she could muster; she was pleased with herself as she handed that to him; she was beginning to enjoy herself, she realised. Eight years ago this man had humiliated and hurt her, but he would never get the chance again. He was dealing with a very different person from the shy, gauche, vulnerable girl he had stood up without a word of explanation, and Nicole meant to make sure he knew it. She had learnt a rigid self-control years ago, and he wouldn't get near her, either mentally or physically; one step too close and she would send him flying.

Frazer looked down into his coffee. 'You parted from Bevis eight years ago, you said?'

'I lost touch with him when I lost touch with Melanie.' She looked along the windowsill at the row of potted plants; pale silvery ivy, a feathery fern which spilled down the side of the earthenware pot, a few plants which carried small pink flowers. Did he look after them? she wondered.

'Did you quarrel?' Frazer asked, and the question bewildered her; she looked back at him, frowning.

'With Bevis? No, I just didn't see him any more— Melanie was my friend, not Bevis.'

Frazer stared at her fixedly; she wondered what was going through his mind; why he was frowning and what was going on behind those hard blue eyes.

'Bevis wasn't your friend,' he repeated as though the simple words had some other meaning, one which defeated her; she couldn't work out why he was staring at her like that. He put down his mug of coffee and turned to stare out into the courtyard, and Nicole absently watched as sunlight gleamed on the faint silvery streak in his thick hair. Eight years ago he had been a powerfully attractive man; she wished she could tell herself the passing of those years had lessened his sexual attraction, had done more than merely touch his black hair with occasional silver and toughen his face into a brown mask. She looked away hurriedly, angry with herself as she realised the involuntary drift of her thoughts. Only a fool would let herself become aware of Frazer Holt in that way, again.

'I'd be grateful if you'd tell Irena Vourlamis that you don't mind if I stay on in her hotel for my full two weeks,' she said, finishing her coffee and putting down the mug.

'Oh, but I do mind,' he said with his back to her, then swung, smiling tightly. 'If you refuse to go, as I said, I can't force you, but you won't find another hotel to take you and the police won't let you camp out.'

On a sudden inspiration she shrugged and said coolly: 'Then I'll go and stay with William Oldfield.'

Frazer's face froze, he stared at her intently. 'Oldfield? You know Oldfield?'

'He has a house with plenty of room in it,' she said, hoping her guess was right. 'I'm sure he'll make me more than welcome.'

Frazer didn't say anything for a moment, but she felt rage emanating from him in waves. When he did speak his lips moved stiffly and his words were tipped with ice.

'I'm sure he will, he likes women.' His eyes ran down over her with a bitter insolence she found intolerable, then he smiled, and it was not a nice smile, it was deliberately contemptuous. 'If he offers you bed and board he means it.' With a shrug he added: 'Of course, if you don't mind paying your way in his bed . . .'

'I can look after myself,' Nicole said ambiguously, and smiled back at him, wondering if William was the type to demand payment in kind rather than money. She hadn't summed him up like that, but of course you never knew with men, he was unlikely to proclaim his sexual attitudes to someone he had only just met. 'Of course, I'd rather stay on with Irena,' she said, because she meant to keep William Oldfield as a last resort, especially now that Frazer had given her a new slant on the man, accurate or not.

'You can't,' Frazer said harshly, and tapped his fingertips on the table, frowning downwards in thought.

Nicole said: 'Oh, well, then . . .' and moved towards the door.

'You'd better stay here,' Frazer said abruptly, and she stopped dead, turning to stare at him incredulously.

'Here?'

'I have plenty of room,' he said, watching her so closely that she had a struggle not to betray what she was thinking. Why was he offering to let her stay in his house? Why didn't he want her to stay with Irena or William—or anyone else, she began to suspect. He had been determined to get her off the island and angry because she was refusing to leave—why should he suddenly invite her to stay with him? The answer was obvious, of course. Frazer had realised that she wasn't going to be scared off easily, so he had decided to keep her under his own eyes where he could make sure she didn't learn too much.

'Well?' he demanded when she was silent, and she managed to hand him a bright smile which was totally false.

'That's very kind of you, thanks. I'd love to stay here.' Frazer might try to interfere with her investigation, he might block all her attempts to find out the truth, but if she was aware of what he was doing she could guard against his manipulation, and merely being here, in the house in which Melanie had been so unhappy, might tell her a good deal. Melanie was dead, and from what she had already seen Frazer had removed anything which might remind him of her, but Nicole felt somehow that her intuition would pick up some vibration from handling objects which Melanie had once handled, sitting in rooms in which Melanie had once sat. This house must surely give her some insight into Melanie's feelings when she lived here.

There were dangers to living here with him, obviously. Nicole's nerves prickled at the idea of seeing so much
of him. She still found him far too attractive, and that
was disturbing; her suspicion about him gave the lance of
agony to those instinctive tugs of attraction. She was
almost beginning to be afraid of what she might find out,
yet she still had to know the truth, as much about herself
and about Melanie as about Frazer. Her mind rang with
confused and painful questions about all of them.

'Come up now and choose which room you'd like,' he
said, turning to the door. She followed him through the
narrow corridor again and up a winding flight of stairs to
an upper floor. Frazer walked along a landing opening
doors and waving a hand towards each room. 'You can
have any of these,' he said, and Nicole glanced into each
in turn, noting that they were more or less indentically
furnished with modern beds and simple oak furniture,
the carpets throughout the whole floor were cream and
the curtains a matt blue weave.

'I sometimes have guests,' said Frazer, as though to
explain why he owned such a large house when he lived
alone. 'My publisher and old buddies from my newspaper fly out for a week from time to time.'

'Does someone come in to do the cleaning?'

'Of course,' he said, opening the last door. 'This is my
room.'

Nicole hovered on the threshold as he walked into the
room; she felt, somehow, that it might not be a good idea
to follow him. The only difference between this room
and the other three was that it was much larger, and in
spite of that more crowded. It looked lived in, whereas
the other rooms had had the tidy impersonality of hotel
rooms; you could tell at once that somebody used this

room, it was full of Frazer's possessions. She saw piles of books everywhere; on the bedside table, on the floor, on shelves on the walls. Flung across the end of the roughly made bed was a white towelling robe, on the floor beside it were black towelling slip-ons with flat soles. On another shelf she saw a pile of tape cassettes and a small tape recorder with headphones lying beside it. A wooden rack held stacked and yellowing newspapers and magazines and a small heap of opened letters had been pushed into one corner of it.

Frazer gave her a wry grin. 'I know, it isn't exactly a showplace.'

She was staring at the bed; wondering if Melanie had shared his room and conscious of a strange dart of sharp emotion at the thought. Here, in this house, she could start to visualise their life together, as she never had until now. It had always seemed unbelievable that Melanie could be Frazer's wife; they had had nothing in common, she had thought, it hadn't really surprised her to be told by Bevis that the marriage hadn't worked out. She hadn't known Frazer for as long as she had known Melanie, there had been a thousand things she did not know about him, but on another level her intuitive sense of the sort of man Frazer was had not needed to know the small details about him. Most people were mosaic made up of so many tiny, contradictory pieces; you could often sense in a few minutes whether you liked the whole picture or not, and only as you got to know them better did you discover everything which went to make up that one, instant impression.

She had known within five minutes of first meeting Frazer that she liked him more than she had ever liked anyone apart from Sam and her parents; her reaction to him had been of a very different order from the way she felt about Sam, of course. It had been complicated by sexuality; even at nineteen she had known that she was sexually aware of Frazer on sight. Now, eight years later, she knew that sexual awareness is not love; it is a subconscious response to someone you could learn to love in the right circumstances. You can call it chemistry, spontaneous combustion, sex appeal—but whatever it's called it is no real guide to the character of the one who causes it because it is instinctive, not rational.

Her feelings about Frazer had not given her any insight into his nature, but she had known Melanie very well for a long, long time, and she had known that they must be opposites. Frazer's idea of a good time was being on a boat fighting the elements, or flying off to war-torn parts of the world to discover the truth, if he could, and write about it. He was clever and quick-witted, tough and cool-headed, a man who was happiest at full stretch, testing himself against danger, taking risks and winning in the face of opposition. That was how she had seen him when they first met; that was the impression he had given her and that was what had attracted her to him. From the minute she met him she had known he was her sort of man, but she had been so young. Had he fooled her? Had she been blinded by her own feelings into believing him her dream man? Had she been in love with Frazer, or only her false image of him?

Melanie's idea of a good time was so different— parties, clothes, flirting and having fun. She hated having her hair blown about in the wind, or getting soaked to the skin on the sea, she was bored by current affairs— unless by that you meant who was sleeping with who— she never told the truth if a lie was easier and she never listened to conversation which went beyond small talk.

Nicole stared at the room, thinking: this bed must have been the only place they really met! And then flinched from that idea, despising herself because she knew she was still half-jealous, she couldn't bear to imagine them in bed together. Perhaps you never quite get over your first love, especially if it has ended badly. Pain clings longer than happiness.

Why had he married Melanie? Had she been totally wrong about him? Had he lied about himself, and what sort of man was he behind that tough, self-contained face?

'I wish I knew what was going on inside your head,' Frazer said, surprising her because he seemed to echo her own thoughts. She had often felt they had some sort of telepathic link, she understood him without speaking, but she had been proved wrong before and maybe she was wrong now.

'I was thinking about Melanie,' she said, meeting his eyes directly.

'Somehow I thought you might be.' His mouth twisted in irony.

'Did she like Mykonos?' If Bevis was screwy and had made a big drama out of one of Melanie's moods, Frazer would answer that unhesitatingly. If he lied, she would know he was hiding something and Bevis's suspicions had good grounds.

Frazer met her eyes directly. 'Not much.' There was a sardonic light in his eyes, as though he was daring her to carry on asking questions and coldly amused because, of course, he could choose which to answer and how to answer them. He had answered that frankly enough. If he had lied it would have been far more revealing.

'She was such a city girl,' Nicole murmured.

'It was too quiet for her here,' he agreed.

'Except in summer, I suppose?'

'Except in summer,' he repeated, and went on smiling, his blue eyes silently telling her: get what you can out of that, much good may it do you.

Nicole was irritated by that smile. She turned up the pressure, her voice still casual.

'How on earth did she come to be spending a night on Delos alone?' Even if she hadn't been watching him so closely she would have felt Frazer's reaction; his body stiffened and his face went wooden, suddenly blank, the smile wiped away as if it had never been there.

'How do you know that?' he asked very quietly, and she shrugged.

'I told you, I have friends in the press . . .'

'The press didn't know about it. Her body was washed up here on Mykonos, it didn't come out that she had been on Delos that night. I had a press cuttings agency send me all the stories which were printed; none of them mentioned Delos.'

'Why shouldn't they?' Nicole felt instinctively that she was getting close to whatever secret he was keeping.

'She shouldn't have been there; the boatman who took her over would have got into serious trouble if it had come out. He knew he was breaking the law.'

'He was from Mykonos?'

Frazer moved away from the window, his hands thrust into his pockets. 'That's obvious,' he said drily. 'You see now why I don't want you prowling around the island asking awkward questions; you'll do more harm than you realise. If you stir up mud, it may stick on innocent people.'

'Innocent people shouldn't be afraid of the truth, surely?' she asked, and he gave a faint sigh, walking out of the room with Nicole on his heels.

'Which bedroom did you decide on?'

She paused at the door of the largest room. 'This one—if that's okay with you?'

'Just as you like.' He shot her a mocking smile over his shoulder. 'You won't be worried about living alone here with me for a few days, of course?'

'Why should I be?' she returned with a cool amusement which she meant him to see.

He laughed shortly. 'Why, indeed? You're obviously capable of dealing with unwanted advances from any man stupid enough to try his luck. Not exactly feminine, but I'm sure it's effective.'

'If I don't fancy someone, he never gets within arm's length,' she murmured deliberately, and Frazer swung away to walk down the stairs. She followed, smiling to herself. Her self-satisfaction was premature. As she reached the foot of the stairs Frazer loomed up behind her from the shadows in the corridor. Nicole had been too preoccupied to be on her guard. Before she knew what was happening, she was held against his body, his forearm, pressing down on her windpipe, his knee forced into the back of her legs. She recognised the hold; if she struggled she knew he could increase the pressure until she blacked out.

There was no point in struggling; her tense body slackened and she let herself go limp against him.

'You were saying?' he mocked.

Nicole shifted one foot, intending to curl it round his ankle and unbalance him, but at once the arm across her throat tightened, pressing down hard.

'Stand still.'

She stood still. 'You're hurting,' she whispered, exaggerating the roughness of her voice.

'Don't try to con me,' Frazer murmured against her ear, his breath warm on her skin. 'I bet you do three rounds with an all-in wrestler every weekend.' His mouth slid from her ear to her neck and she tensed, nerves prickling. He pulled her back even closer so that she felt his body touching her from shoulder to calf, at the same time sliding his fingers lightly upwards, following the curve of her body up to her breast.

Nicole shuddered, teeth gritted.

'Now throw me over your shoulder,' Frazer mocked.

'I can wait,' Nicole muttered through her clenched teeth. 'I'll get my chance sooner or later.'

She felt laughter shake him, the chest behind her back was lifting and falling with it.

'My God, I believe you,' he said, a smile in his voice. 'I've been threatened by hulking brutes before now and never turned a hair, but you scare me, Nicole—you make it all sound very personal. I'd like to know what happened to you to give you this edge—you glitter like a razor blade, and I'm damned sure you're just as deadly.'

She heard him with disbelief. Didn't he know what he'd done to her? Had he forgotten all about that last date? All these years she had been hating him because he had humiliated her, and Frazer had forgotten the whole thing. That should have made her feel less wound up, but it didn't; it deepened her humiliation. She had mattered so little to him and he had mattered so much to her—that thought sliced into her and made her bleed inwardly.

'Was it Bevis?' he asked, but she barely heard the

words because he was kissing her neck and she was rigid with awareness of that fact. Her skin was burning, she tried to break away while his attention was elsewhere, but it seemed he could concentrate on two things at once, because as soon as she made that sharp move his arm clamped down hard and she gave a strangled gasp.

'I thought I told you to stand still?' She stood stiffly, bitterly conscious of the caressing hand exploring the length of her body and the warmth of his body pressing into her back. 'Take some well-meant advice, Nicole,' he murmured, softly brushing his lips along her nape. 'Forget about Melanie, enjoy your holiday. Don't make waves which could swamp everyone around you.' He tightened his arm again. 'Are you listening?'

'Yes,' she said with icy rage. How could she help but listen?

'A pity you cut your hair, I liked it long; I used to fantasise about winding it round and round your neck like a silver collar.' His arm lifted from her throat but before she could move away his hand softly stroked upward from her shoulder to her lifted chin. 'I could have strangled you with that hair,' he whispered.

'Sorry, you'll have to use your bare hands,' she muttered, and managed then to detach herself and swing to face him. Their eyes met; his mocking, gleaming with self-satisfaction and her own dark with anger. His hard mouth was curling in a smile which only intensified her rage; Frazer had won that round and he knew it. She had thrown him a defiant challenge and she had been too sure of herself; she had lost.

Nicole pulled herself together, swallowing. 'I'll go round and see Irena, pack my things and pay her.'

He nodded, his voice husky as he said: 'Leave the case

with her, I'll pick it up later.' He opened the door into the courtyard for her and walked with her to the gate, but didn't say a thing on the way. Before he closed the gate on her again, though, he said: 'I'm having lunch with someone. Can you eat before you come back here? I'll be back myself around four.'

'See you at four, then,' Nicole said as lightly as she could, and walked away. The sun was high in the blue sky; it must be noon and some of the shops were already closing for the afternoon siesta; they would re-open around three o'clock, she knew from past experience.

Irena was at the reception desk when she went into the small hotel. She looked up, her eyes alert, but before Nicole could say anything, Irena said: 'Frazer rang just now to explain that you were going to stay with him. I'm sorry if you have been inconvenienced.' It was a stilted little speech and far from friendly; Irena clearly had not changed her attitude since that morning.

'I'll pack and leave my case with you. Frazer will pick it up later,' Nicole said, and the other woman nodded.

Nicole went upstairs and felt Irena's cold eyes on her back. How well had Irena known Melanie? There was no point in asking her, of course; Irena would die rather than tell her anything.

As Nicole packed she methodically added up all she knew about Melanie's death and looked for some answer to the riddle, but clearly there were too many missing pieces from the jigsaw at the moment, and how was she going to locate those pieces when nobody wanted to answer questions?

She left her case standing in her room and went downstairs to pay Irena. There was no one at the reception desk now. Nicole went to the door which led to the family quarters. She was about to knock on it when she heard Frazer's voice behind it and her hand froze in mid-air.

'It seemed the only solution.'

'Why can't you frighten her away like that other one?' That was Irena's voice, she sounded on edge, her tone high and shaky.

'Nicole doesn't scare so easily,' Frazer drawled as though it amused him, and Nicole wasn't sure she liked that.

'She's only a girl!' Irena spoke with harsh impatience, angry now. 'You men are all the same!'

'Irena,' Frazer said in a very different voice, and Nicole listened with a frown. She heard a movement, a soft sound like a kiss, and her face hardened. A kiss? Had Frazer kissed Irena—and why? Irena was married to a fisherman called Paul who was away at the moment. What was going on between her and Frazer?

'Can't you see how dangerous this could be for us?' Irena whispered so huskily that Nicole became certain that Frazer had kissed her; her voice held so much emotion.

'Trust me,' Frazer said very gently. 'I'd better go before she catches sight of me,' he added, and Nicole heard a movement, a footstep behind the door. She turned and lightly, softly, fled back to the stairs. Halfway down them she turned and waited until she heard Frazer walking across the lobby, then she came down the stairs just as Irena emerged with a handkerchief in her hands as if she had just dried her eyes with it. She looked up, and there were shadows under her eyes. Nicole gave her a polite smile.

'I've come to pay my bill.'

Irena pushed the bill across the desk without a word. Nicole looked at the total, which was very small. She counted out the drachma notes, and Irena took them and pushed them into a till on the desk.

'I've left my case in my room; I'll bring it down in a minute.'

'No need,' Irena said shortly. 'Frazer can get it when he comes later.'

Casually, Nicole said: 'I thought I saw him going out of the door just now—he could have got my case then.'

Irena didn't answer. She was pretending to be busy tidying the desk. Nicole shot her a quick, observant look. Yes, Irena had been crying; her lids were pink and her lashes had stuck together where her mascara had run.

'Well, I hope I'll see you again,' she said, turning towards the door, but Irena did not take any notice. She walked away towards her private quarters and vanished.

CHAPTER SIX

NICOLE walked down to the waterfront and sat down at a table in front of one of the tavernas. She chose a different one this time; the waiter looked rather more friendly. The menu was chalked up on a board hanging beside the door. From the shade of a red striped umbrella, Nicole studied it and ordered chicken soup flavoured with lemon followed by squid served with rice; although the taverna did a few meat dishes it was basically a fish restaurant, and its specialities would be much better.

The waiter brought her the bottle of retsina she had ordered before he came with the soup, and while she waited Nicole sipped the smoky resin-flavoured wine and stared out across the blue horizon. A heat haze hung over the sea in the direction of Delos, which was half an hour's sailing away. She must take a trip over there one morning; she wanted to see the beach from which Melanie had swum out for the last time.

Her mind moved on to the murmured conversation she had overheard between Frazer and Irena. It hadn't entered Nicole's head until that moment that Irena and Frazer might have some more intimate relationship than the casual friendship of people who lived in a small town on a remote island. Was that why Frazer had insisted that she couldn't stay at Irena's hotel? Had he been afraid she would discover what was going on between them? Irena's husband was a fisherman, always away from home, it wouldn't be hard to keep such a secret from him, or wouldn't he mind? It couldn't be easy to have an affair in a place like Mykonos—people knew you too well, saw too much, gossiped too much.

Then she remembered something else—Irena had asked Frazer why he couldn't just frighten her away, as he had the other one. Had Irena meant Bevis? Or the detective he had sent from Athens? But that would mean that their affair had been going on while Melanie was alive!

She sat upright, her hand clenched on her wine glass, pale and frowning. How long had the affair been going on? Was that why Melanie had been so unhappy and wanted to get away? Was it the root cause of her death? Had Melanie drowned deliberately, had she killed herself? Or . . .

She broke off the question which had begun to form itself in her mind, biting her inner lip. No, Frazer just wasn't the type to murder his wife because she resented his affair with another woman. Nicole could imagine circumstances in which Frazer might lose his temper and become violent; but she couldn't imagine him coldbloodedly planning to get rid of his wife.

The waiter brought her bowl of chicken soup and some hot pitta to eat with it. She bit off a mouthful of the charcoal-burnt bread absentmindedly, her head bent and her soft silvery hair whipping around her face. A wind had sprung up from the sea, she heard the mast wires of boats jangling along the harbour wall.

She had come here believing that she could guess what lay behind Melanie's death; she had been angry with Frazer because he had made Melanie unhappy by forcing her to live on an island far away from everything she knew and enjoyed, but it hadn't even entered her head that Frazer had given Melanie other causes for unhappiness. She had wondered if Melanie might have been unfaithful to him—never if he had been unfaithful to Melanie.

A soft footstep behind her made her turn her head, startled. Adoni smiled at her, his dark eyes lustrous.

'Hallo, Adoni,' said Nicole, relaxing. Her nerves must be in a bad way, she had felt quite edgy for a second as she sensed someone behind her.

'Hallo, Nicole,' Adoni said carefully, then grinned with triumph at having got that out without mistake. 'Good?' he asked, looking at the soup she was tasting.

'Very good,' she said. 'Sit down and talk to me.'

Adoni accepted without hesitation. She pushed the plate of pitta towards him, raising her fine brows. 'Want some?'

'Thank you,' he said, taking it between thin brown fingers and breaking it with an almost hypnotic deliberation which was ritualistic, she felt.

Nicole looked at him through her lashes, smiling. 'Did you tell Frazer Holt that I was here?'

Adoni's face was pure innocence; he looked at her, wide-eyed. 'Miss?'

'I bet you did. A friend of yours, is he?' she waited, but Adoni didn't answer.

Adoni ate his bread and she drank her soup. 'He's a friend of *mine*,' she said. 'I'm moving into his house for my stay here.'

Adoni looked unsurprised. 'Yes,' he said simply.

Nicole laughed. 'Is there anything you don't know?' If only she could get him to talk, heaven knows what she'd find out, she thought, but one look into those dark wells of eyes told her she would need to use a thumbscrew on

Adoni to get him to tell her anything he decided she should not know. Or anything Frazer decided she should not know? Did it come to the same thing? Frazer had quite a pull here—was it because he was so rich and famous? Or because he spoke fluent Greek and they all liked him?

The waiter came out to take her soup bowl and place in front of her an enormous dish of squid cooked in peppers, tomatoes and onions and served on a bed of boiled rice. He also brought a small bowl of green salad tossed in olive oil and lemon juice. Giving Adoni a grin, he said something to him in Greek and Adoni threw back a rapid mutter, laughing.

'What was all that about?' Nicole asked, taking some of the salad.

'He said you very pretty,' Adoni said mischievously.

'Well, tell him I'm flattered,' said Nicole, then caught a puzzled look in his eyes and changed that to: 'Say thank you for me.'

Adoni laughed and rattled off another sentence. The waiter gave her a smiling bow, kissed his fingers and went back into the taverna.

A shadow fell over the table and looking up Nicole saw William Oldfield standing next to her. 'You shouldn't eat salad or fruit,' he told her. 'It's been washed in the local water and may give you tummy trouble.'

'It never bothers me,' Nicole said, taking some more salad.

Adoni got up. 'Goodbye, Nicole,' he said, ignoring William, and darted off. William took his chair while Nicole stared after Adoni. So *he* didn't like William, either? Now why shouldn't he?

'Did you find Holt's house?' William asked.

'Yes.' Nicole ate some squid; it was delicious and the sauce it had been cooked in was mouthwatering. She looked up a moment later. 'He asked me to stay with him while I was on the island.' Sooner or later William would hear about that, she might as well be the one to tell him. Or wouldn't he hear? Did the people here talk to him? Or did they just ignore him, the way Adoni had just done?

William stared at her, his mouth turning down at the edges. It was a rather thin mouth, she realised; slightly petulant, the lines around it all went downward. His face was immature, it had a boyish look when you first saw it until you noticed the other little details of it; the pale eyes which were deep-set below narrow temples, the pinched look of the thin nostrils and that sulky mouth.

'You didn't say he was a friend of yours, I thought you were just curious because he was famous.'

'I knew him years ago,' she said. 'Before he started writing.'

'Did you know his wife too?' That was a sneer, she realised, and looked at him directly, her face cold.

'I did, actually, she was a childhood friend of mine.'

'She was man-mad, wasn't she? That's what I heard from friends of mine in Athens; she and Holt used to spend a few weeks there every year and she always started up a flirtation with somebody while she was there.' He was staring at Nicole with a malicious smile on that thin mouth, and she was deciding that she could well understand why nobody on Mykonos liked him. William's first impression on her had been quite pleasant, but that was rapidly wearing off.

'Melanie was very lively,' she said, hearing herself

with surprise because she was defending Melanie, resenting the criticism of her. Melanie hadn't been able to help her own character; she had always enjoyed flirting with people, she had needed that constant jab of adrenalin, she got bored when life became routine and quiet. Even Melanie's act of treachery to her suddenly became forgivable, as she looked back at it and realised how inevitable it had been. Melanie was a magpie; she had been attracted to Frazer precisely because she knew how Nicole felt about him; that had made him alluring to Melanie, she had been driven to steal him away, and, with childlike inability to understand other people, she had not expected Nicole to be angry for long.

If their positions had been reversed, Nicole saw suddenly, Melanie would have forgiven her, because Melanie had never felt any deep emotion, she floated over the surface of life, bright and glittering and without any idea of the depths of the dark sea below her. The day Melanie asked her to be her bridesmaid should have enlightened her about how Melanie's mind worked. Melanie had been extending a hand, expecting indulgent forgiveness, knowing that she had annoyed Nicole but not realising how bitterly Nicole felt about it. As Melanie saw it, she had gaily stolen a toy from Nicole; it had been a game to her, she had probably laughed happily as she ran off with Frazer and she hadn't guessed for a second that it would divide the two of them for ever. They had had such different natures—if it had not been for the accident of meeting in childhood they would probably never have become friends in the first place, they had been opposites, but opposites attract sometimes. Wasn't that the secret of infatuation? The lover sees in the beloved what he knows he doesn't possess himself; the quiet thoughtful man is often drawn to the gay, thoughtless woman. The driving compulsion of such an affair is based entirely on the gulf between the lovers, and Nicole saw that her friendship with Melanie had been based on her own envy of Melanie's lighthearted approach to life, her popularity and sunny good temper. Did she have any right to blame Melanie for the very qualities which had drawn her in the first place?

Was that what had drawn Fraser, too? Had he begun to blame Melanie later? Had he tired of her rapidly once he knew her better?

William sat in silence while Nicole ate her lunch and thought about the past with much more clarity. When she had finished and pushed her plate away, he leaned over and said: 'If you're having coffee now, I'll have some, unless you'd prefer me to go.' He sounded sulky, he looked sulky, but Nicole gave him a wry smile.

'Yes, do have some coffee. Would you call the waiter?' She did not want to offend him; he might be able to tell her more about Melanie's life here. He turned and called and the waiter came and took away her plate. William ordered coffee for them both.

'I ate at home,' he told Nicole, who nodded. 'I spent the morning working.'

'Are you writing at the moment?'

'I was revising my book on Mykonos; it goes off soon, to London, to my agent there, then I must start thinking about my next book, I suppose.' He didn't look as though that prospect excited him.

'Will you have to move on to another island to write it?'

He shrugged. 'No, I'm going to do Tinos and Andros

next; both in one book. I write very short books; it's the pictures that are the most important. I enjoy taking photographs.' He didn't look as though he enjoyed doing anything very much as he stared up at the sky, shading his eyes. 'I'll stay on Mykonos for as long as I can; the rent on my house here is so small, I wouldn't find anything cheaper elsewhere.'

Nicole smiled, listening, sipping the coffee which had arrived. William talked about himself, his work, his boat, his family in England and his voice became a soft drone like the buzzing of a wasp around her head; she felt sleepy after the glasses of retsina and the delicious food, the sun was so hot and her head so heavy she felt her eyelids drooping and had to jerk herself awake, taking a long drink of strong, black, extra-sweet Greek coffee; the dregs of it like river mud, thick and glutinous. She called the waiter over from another table and asked for some more coffee. 'Not so sweet,' she said in English, and William put it into halting Greek for her. The waiter smiled and nodded.

Nicole leaned back, her chair creaking, her eye wandered along the harbour and then stopped on a face she recognised even at this distance. Irena Vourlamis was standing at the far end of the quayside. She was in a pink blouse and white pleated skirt, her black hair blown by the wind, and she was alone as Nicole first saw her, but a moment later a man joined her. Nicole watched him kissing Irena. He was wearing a loose white shirt and black trousers. She couldn't see his face, but she saw his black hair, the width of his shoulders and his height and for a flash of time she thought it was Frazer, then he and Irena began to walk towards her and as he moved she knew it wasn't Frazer.

'So you haven't been there?' William was saying, and she looked round at him, lost in thought.

'Been where?' she asked absently, then saw his offended face and realised she had given away that she had not been listening to him. From somewhere her mind pulled back the memory of him mentioning Delos and she added quickly: 'Oh, Delos? Well, only years ago, I just about remember it.'

'You must sail over, you can't miss Delos; it's one of the most wonderful places in the Greek world. Why don't I take you over in my boat one day this week? How about the day after tomorrow? We could take a picnic and spend a whole afternoon there. Will you come?'

'Thank you, I'd love to,' she said. After all, she had been meaning to go over in her own boat and it would help to have William with her, he could tell her exactly where Melanie's clothes had been found. She had a strong feeling he would know.

She glanced back towards where Irena and the man were walking. William was talking again, but he broke off as he saw where she was staring. The man had an arm round Irena's slim waist and she was leaning against his shoulder, her face alight with happiness. It wasn't just a smile, although she *was* smiling; it was the look of a contentment you very rarely saw on anyone's face, and Nicole was puzzled and startled by it. If Irena was having an affair with Frazer, she wouldn't look like that when she was with another man. Would she? And who was this other man? Nicole assessed him, her green eyes narrowed. Very good-looking, she decided; tall and lithe with a deep tan and a chiselled profile, a long straight nose, firm mouth and black eyes. He was almost too spectacularly attractive; he didn't look quite real.

'So he's back,' William remarked beside her, and she looked round at him.

'Who is he?'

'One of the local fisherman,' William said with one of his petulant little sneers. 'All the girls moon after him, he's the local Don Juan, but when he's fishing he's away for days at a time.'

'Is that his wife?' Nicole asked, but she knew the answer before William nodded. So that was why Irena had told her to leave the hotel—she had not wanted Nicole around because Paul Vourlamis was coming home and she had not wanted Nicole to ask him any embarrassing questions about Frazer. Did Paul Vourlamis know that his wife was involved with Frazer? Or was Irena merely making sure he did not find out?

'I must go,' she told William, getting up. She looked around for the waiter who materialised with her bill. She paid him and added a generous tip, she wanted to make sure he welcomed her back again.

'Do we have a date for the day after tomorrow?' William asked, and she nodded, smiling.

'I'll look forward to it. What time shall I meet you?'

'Noon here on the waterfront? My boat's called *Agathi*; it's the blue and white one over there—see it?' He pointed and she glanced in that direction, nodding. 'I'll meet you there,' William said. 'Noon. Don't forget.'

Nicole walked slowly through the glaringly white streets, the brazen stroke of the sun on the back of her neck. The shops were re-opening, cats lay curled up in the sunshine, the smell of cooked fish still hovered on the air, and somewhere a bell was ringing, as it always was here on Mykonos. She paused to stare at a display of local pottery in a shop; bright blue bowls on which painted yellow dolphins curved, flat black plates with orange figures of Greek warriors on them, white dishes with black owls in the centre, all the traditional designs of octopi and fish and birds, replicas of ancient Greek pottery. She must take some home to Sam, but she would compare prices before she chose.

When she got back to Frazer's house the gate was open, and she halted just inside it, seeing Frazer himself in the courtyard. He had his back to her, walking across the sunlit stone, his black shadow thrown in bold relief behind him. Nicole felt a sharp jab of pain as she watched him; she did not want to feel anything but contempt and anger and her own weakness infuriated her. He puzzled her: she seemed to see two separate and distinct personalities, one the man she had met on that holiday in the Hebrides long ago, the man she had fallen in love with so intensely, the man who was intelligent and charming, gentle and tough, direct and shrewd—and this other man, who had dropped her without a word when he decided he preferred Melanie, who had some sort of secret affair with Irena Vourlamis, who had threatened Bevis and his detective and driven them both away. Which was the real Frazer? Or was he a split personality? Did all the contradictory pieces of him fit, after all? Was one the negative side of the other?

He suddenly turned, as though becoming aware of her, and she walked towards him trying to look relaxed and casual, although she was on edge and very nervous about being alone with him. It was rare for her to feel uneasy with a man—she was usually certain of her own ability to handle the opposite sex and she didn't enjoy the novelty of her unusual wariness.

His black hair had taken on a blue gleam in the sunlight. 'Did you have a good lunch?'

'Yes, thanks, delicious; I ate in a taverna on the waterfront.' She sat down on a white-painted wooden seat under the mulberry tree, in cool moving shade. 'I feel rather sleepy now; too much retsina.' She smiled politely; this was small talk of the kind one exchanges with a stranger, but Frazer Holt was no stranger. She hadn't known him for very long, but she had already felt she had known him very well. You can't measure depth of feeling by time, and Nicole's bitterness about Frazer had given a painful intimacy to how she felt about him.

He sat down beside her and flung back his head, relaxing, his eyes half-shut, his golden-brown skin gleaming in the light.

'I've collected your case—I put it in your room. Go up whenever you like. While you're here, you're free to come and go as you choose. A local woman comes in and cleans the house, but I'd be grateful if you'd make your bed each morning.'

'Of course. Anthing else I can do . . .'

'Do you cook?' Frazer asked, turning his head to watch her through those half-closed lids, his eyes a veiled blue glitter.

'I'm quite a good cook. Shall I make supper tonight to show you?'

'There's a fresh lobster in a tank in the kitchen,' said Frazer, and she drew a startled breath.

'No!' she said with a shudder. 'I couldn't—not lobster.'

He grinned, his eyes opening wide, very blue. 'Okay, I was only pulling your leg. There isn't any lobster. I remembered how horrified you used to be about the way lobster was cooked, and I wondered if you'd changed.'

'No, I haven't,' she answered aggressively, her chin up, because she resented him mentioning the past; which was stupid, because why else was she here except to find out the answers to questions about the past which troubled her?

'I'm glad you haven't altered that much,' Frazer remarked lazily, his hands in his pockets and his long, lean body at rest against the seat. He swung one foot idly, his legs crossed at the knee, and she stared at it.

'Did Melanie change much?' She saw his foot stop swinging.

'No.' He seemed to have nothing to add to that blanket denial.

'She was such fun—so lighthearted and full of energy.' Nicole found she was seeing Melanie much more clearly now; during the years between the marriage and the day she met Bevis in the dark street a few nights ago, she had lost Melanie, Melanie had become her enemy. Now she had cancelled out the injury Melanie had dealt her when she married Frazer and she could remember Melanie with love and warmth again.

Frazer stood up. 'She was reckless, restless, selfish and blind to everything but her own feelings,' he said flatly. 'Or don't you remember her as well as you seem to think you do?' He turned and walked across the courtyard into the house, and Nicole stared after him. Although he spoke so levelly she had picked up the bitterness behind the voice, not so much from his face as from the tension in his body.

After a few moments she got up, too, and walked into the house, feeling the coolness of the shadowy stone dropping over her after the hot glare of the sun, a sigh of pleasure coming from her as she moved slowly down the corridor.

She walked quietly up the stairs and as she reached the landing saw Frazer through the open door of his bedroom, pulling off his shirt, his bare chest very tanned, the smooth expanse of his skin roughened with curly black hairs down the centre. The muscles in shoulder and arm rippled as he threw the shirt on the bed. He began to take off the belt of the light blue pants he wore and Nicole quickly moved into her own room. There was no lock on the door, she discovered, which bothered her. She stood a chair against it and took off her own clothes to take a shower in the narrow cubicle in the corner of the room.

She stood under the cool jets of water, eyes closed, face lifted, revelling in the feel of the refreshing spray hitting her skin. When she had washed off all the dust and perspiration of the hot day she stepped out and wrapped herself in a large white towel. She sat in front of the dressing-table, combing her wet hair back from her face, listening for sounds of movement from Frazer without hearing a thing.

He must have cared deeply about Melanie to be so bitter about her. That hadn't been assumed, that black feeling she had got from him earlier. Frazer was bitter; what had Melanie done to him? Flirted with other men? That wouldn't surprise Nicole; she was certain Melanie had done that, she couldn't have changed much, either. People don't, she thought. Melanie had never had any depth of feeling, how could she ever learn to feel deeply for Frazer?

Why had Melanie been on that beach at night? Why had she drowned when she could swim like a fish?

Melanie had never cared much for sport, but swimming had been one sport she had enjoyed and she had been good at it.

Frazer's reluctance to talk about her death proved that there was something about it which he wanted to stay hidden—but what was it?

She was so absorbed in her own thoughts that she didn't hear someone trying the door handle; the first she knew was that the door had opened and the chair leaning against it had crashed down sideways, making her jump.

In the mirror her startled, angry green eyes met Frazer's blue gaze. He was leaning in the open doorway, watching her.

'Sorry to wreck your barricade,' he said with sarcasm. 'If you give me warning in future, I won't come in here.'

'You might have knocked.'

'I did,' he said shortly, and she believed him, or rather, she believed the hardening of his mouth and the flash of the blue eyes.

'I was so hot, I took a shower,' she explained, looking back over her shoulder to avoid seeing her own reflection and being reminded that all she wore was a towel. It was stupid to feel selfconscious; she wore less on a beach and the towel was very big, it covered her from her breasts to her knees.

Frazer moved lazily towards her and she tensed, her hand gripping the hairbrush. Looking back at the mirror she saw her own smooth, golden shoulders and naked arms, her hair, darkened with water, slicked back from her damp face, her eyes full of an instinctive excitement she did not want to recognise, the green far too bright, the pupils far too large.

Swallowing, she said: 'Paul Vourlamis is an incredibly good-looking man, isn't he?'

Frazer halted, looming behind her. In the mirror she saw his brows jerk together. 'Where did you see him?'

'He landed on the waterfront while I was eating my lunch.'

'How did you know it was Paul?'

'William told me.'

'You had lunch with Oldfield?' That didn't seem to please him much, either, his frown deepened. 'Did you know him before you came to Mykonos?'

Nicole casually lifted the brush to her hair to smooth back one wet strand which had fallen against her cheek, but the movement dislodged her towel, which slipped down from her breasts. She hurriedly dropped the brush with a clatter on to the dressing-table and tugged at the towel to hide the full pale gold flesh, the hard pink nipples, angrily aware of Frazer's eyes riveted on them.

'No,' she said, her voice breathless. 'I only met William here.' She changed the subject hurriedly. 'Irena met her husband on the quay—I can't remember when I last saw a man that striking; his looks are almost film-starish, aren't they?'

'Irena's a very jealous woman. Don't let her see you looking at her husband,' Frazer said brusquely, and she gave him a thoughtful look.

'And him? Is he jealous, too?'

Frazer's eyes were blank. He didn't reply, and Nicole laughed softly. No doubt that would make him wonder how much she had already learnt, how much she had guessed, about his own relationship with Irena!

From the faint dampness of his black hair she guessed that he, too, had had a shower. He had changed his clothes, and was now wearing black jeans and a white shirt which was open at the neck, revealing his tanned throat.

'I can't imagine Melanie living in this house,' she said. 'I can't see her putting up with life on Mykonos. Why did you insist on living here? Why not Athens?'

His mouth tightened. 'You ask too many damned questions,' he muttered, and his hands clamped down over her shoulders and pulled her backwards, tilting her body towards him without allowing her to struggle to her feet.

Her eyes restlessly flickered upwards, given a glimpse of his inverted face, dark, tensely set, then his mouth swooped down and took her by surprise; the impact of the first brush of it sending a wild shudder through her which she knew he must have felt and comprehended, because the fingers gripping her bare shoulders relaxed a little, his thumbs moving softly, strokingly, on her damp skin.

She felt giddy, dizzy; her eyes closed tightly against that sudden emotional vertigo and her lips opened in helpless response. Frazer's hands slowly slid down her arms and covered her breasts; the towel peeled gently down and she gave a muffled moan of half protest, half pleasure as his cool fingers closed over her flesh.

For years she had had a barrier inside her head; excluding all the men she met, rejecting love because it had betrayed her when she was too young to know how to get over the pain of being rejected. Behind that self-erected barrier over the years all her instinctive emotions had built up; passion and desire, need and sensuality. Frazer's sensitive fingers had broken down that barrier and the tidal waters came crashing through her with a force which made her blind to everything but her own responses.

His mouth teased and tantalised, lifting away briefly and returning with a demand she met without reservation. He slid a hand under her knees and lifted her up into his arms. She slid her own hands round his neck, her mouth lifted to search for his and finding it with a husky groan of satisfaction.

He walked with her to the bed and laid her on it, kneeling beside her, still kissing her. She felt his fingers unwrap the towel and then his hands were moving in a slow, sensuous exploration of her body while she shivered with desire and excitement and kissed his mouth passionately.

She felt one of his hands lift away from her and heard him undoing his shirt, then he knelt up, unzipping his jeans, and Nicole opened her eyes. It was an effort; her lids felt heavy, weighted with drowsy desire, she felt a deep burning hunger inside her; her body was aching with unsatisfied need.

Frazer was watching her, his skin tight over his cheekbones, his mouth unsteady and a hard flush on his face.

Her mind began working. She tried to halt it, she did not want to think, that was the last thing she wanted to do, but she couldn't stop the rapid process.

'Why do I ask too many questions?' she whispered. 'Why don't you want to answer them?' Frazer stiffened, staring at her, and she was feeling cold suddenly; she pulled the towel back over her and looked at him bitterly.

'How did Melanie die? Why did Melanie die?' she asked him with the force of her own pain and disillusionment behind the words.

Frazer zipped up his jeans again. He pulled on his shirt and did it up, and then he got off the bed, all without saying a word. He looked down at her, his hostile gaze running from her tumbled damp silver-blonde hair to the warm, feminine curve of her half-naked body.

'You'll never know,' he said harshly, then he turned and walked out of the room, slamming the door behind him.

CHAPTER SEVEN

SHE lay on the bed, aching with frustration, tears prickling behind her lowered lids. Nicole always had to know the truth, however much it hurt, she needed to know, she found it too humiliating to allow herself to stay blind.

Frazer had been making love to her to distract her from her questions about Melanie. His only motive for everything he had done since she arrived on Mykonos had been to stop her finding out what had really happened on that night two years ago. He had tried to frighten her away, he had arranged for her to be turned out of her hotel, he had invited her to stay with him and pretended to be attracted to her—all for the same reason, and that meant that he must have a very strong motive in wanting to hide the truth.

If there had been nothing strange about Melanie's death, why would he want to silence all questions about it?

Rolling off the bed, she took off the towel and dressed; small white panties, a matching bra, jeans and a dark green shirt which had long, gauzy sleeves, very full until they narrowed into the wrist and fastened with two little silver buttons. It gave her a crisply efficient look, slightly Victorian in a tailored way. She brushed her drying hair into drifting silvery strands around her face; outlined her lips in coral and lightly smoothed green over her lids. Her tanned face needed no foundation; her skin was clear and healthy.

She unpacked and hung clothes in the wardrobe, pushed them neatly into drawers in the matching chest and arranged her cosmetics and toilet articles on the dressing-table. While she was doing that she was taking in the details of the room more intently, but there was nothing here that she felt had belonged to Melanie; it was just like a hotel room, an acceptable shell holding nothing which echoed the past.

She went out, closing the door very softly, and listened for sounds from downstairs. She heard music; Mahler, she thought, brows lifting. Moving on the balls of her feet, she went into the other two empty rooms and walked around them inspecting everything; they were just as unrevealing and impersonal as the one she was using.

What had he done with all Melanie's things? Had he sold them? Given them away? Destroyed them?

She hesitated at his bedroom door, turned her head to listen again. She didn't want him to catch her prowling around his room; Frazer was more unpredictable than she liked. She had a feeling he might be a lot more dangerous than she had imagined, too. Glancing over the banisters she saw that the corridor below was empty; the door from behind which the music came was closed. She walked quietly into his bedroom and began to open cupboards and drawers. She found his clothes, his underwear neatly stacked, his socks and handkerchiefs, ties hanging in a row, shirts crisply ironed. Books everywhere; a few letters and pages of manuscript. The room was full of Frazer—but it held nothing of Melanie.

Her trained eye noted a great many details; his shirts had a good label in them, his shoes were expensively handmade and his jackets and suits were immaculately tailored and well kept. Frazer had money—but then she had known that already.

She picked up the letters and glanced through them; one of them was a personal letter, brief and cheerful, from someone who had obviously worked with Frazer on his newspaper. The others were all business letters; two of them from a publisher's office, another handful of them bills.

Nicole went over to shut the wardrobe door and just as she did so her eye caught a blue leather corner sticking out from under a pile of cotton t-shirts on an upper shelf. She carefully lifted the shirts and took down the large, square leather-bound book. It was a photograph album.

She stiffened, a frisson of excitement running through her, then heard a movement downstairs. The door had opened, the Mahler was louder. She pushed the wardrobe door shut and silently tiptoed out of the room, the album under her arm. She went into her own room, pushing the door closed behind her, and hid the album under her mattress, arranging the bedclothes so that there should be no sign of the mattress having been lifted.

She straightened to move away and heard a tap at the door. She walked over without haste and opened it, her face politely cool.

'If you want to eat here, I'm eating cold lamb and salad,' said Frazer, and his eyes rested guardedly on her as though unsure what he would see. 'You're welcome to share it.'

'Thank you, that sounds fine.'

He turned away and she followed; she would rather have stayed in her room to examine the album, but she would have to leave that for a time when she could be certain of being uninterrupted. It would have to be tonight—Frazer might notice that the album had gone and he wouldn't need to spend much time working out who had taken it. She must get it back into its hiding place as soon as possible.

'We must discuss what arrangement to make about this,' she said to the back of Frazer's neck as they went down the stairs. 'I can't stay here for nothing.'

'You're my guest,' he said shortly.

'I'd prefer to keep it on a business footing.'

'Well, I wouldn't.' He went into the kitchen, the table was laid for two and in the centre of it stood a bowl of dressed salad, a basket of bread and a large platter of thick, sliced cold lamb. Nicole glanced at her watch. It was seven o'clock; the sun had sunk in the sky and the air had a chill on it. Out in the courtyard the shadows had deepened and moths were flitting around the mulberry tree and tapping at the closed windows of the house. Frazer was opening a bottle of Greek wine with practised deftness, he poured a little into a glass and tasted it.

'Nicely chilled,' he said, and filled both glasses on the table. 'Sit down and help yourself.'

Nicole lifted some of the salad with the wooden salad servers and put it on her plate, took a slice of lamb and a piece of newly baked bread. The meal was simple, but although she had had such a large lunch she found herself quite hungry and she enjoyed the food.

'How's Sam these days?' asked Frazer, sipping his golden wine.

'He's fine, he hasn't changed except that he's older. He rarely sails now; he works too hard, I'm always trying to persuade him to take it easier, but he prefers to be busy.'

'Are you a full partner now? You seem to be good at the job; you must be a terror to insurance swindlers; does Sam let you do most of the fieldwork?' He was eating mostly salad, as she was; it had a crisp, delicious flavour and texture and was very refreshing.

'I do all the jobs which involve travelling. Sam stays in the office, he does most of the paperwork, his brain is as good as ever, but he tires quickly.'

'You're still very fond of him,' Frazer commented drily.

'Did you think I wouldn't be? I owe Sam more than I can ever repay; he's like a father to me.'

'I've never noticed that owing people something necessarily makes one fond of them,' Frazer said with a cynical little smile, and her eyes hardened.

'No? Well, I love Sam dearly and I don't forget how much I owe him. I know I can trust him with my life, and that's something very special.'

'Yes, it is,' said Frazer on a different note, his blue eyes staring deep into her own as though trying to push behind what she was saying to what she was thinking. Nicole stared back at him and wished *she* could see inside *his* head; she still couldn't make him out, be certain which of the two separate images was the real Frazer Holt. Once she had thought she could trust him the way she trusted Sam; she had learnt otherwise and in the process got very hurt. She was older and much tougher; she wasn't going to expose herself to pain again, but her own honesty forced her to admit that if there was a man who could affect her deeply enough to be able to hurt her, it was this man. The danger was that she wanted to trust him, she wanted to stop guarding herself against him. Every time she was with him she was aware of a bitter tug of attraction; if she wasn't careful she could fall in love with him all over again, in spite of the past experience of him.

'Are there any men in your life?' Frazer asked, looking down at his plate.

'That's a very personal question.'

'You fire personal questions at me every two minutes,' he pointed out with a dry smile.

'And you never answer them!'

'You don't ask questions I *can* answer.'

'Tell me some you can, then!'

He smiled, his blue eyes mocking her. 'Ask me if I think you're beautiful, ask me if I'd like to go to bed with you—I'll answer like a shot!'

She laughed, her mouth curling upwards, cynical disbelief in her eyes. 'Oh, sure you would—but would it be the truth?'

'You want truth? You're either an idealistic romantic or a halfwit. In this world you might as well cry for the moon. If I knew the truth, I couldn't tell it to you, it would take me too long. I'd have to weigh up every tiny fragment of evidence I knew and then hedge it around with ifs and buts—what the hell does the word truth mean, Nicole? If you know, tell me. I'd give my right arm to have that definition.'

She stared at him, surprised by his harsh outburst. He met her eyes and stopped talking, shrugged wryly, then went on in a dry voice.

'Sorry. Look, if your questions only related to me I'd answer them, but there are others involved who might get hurt; innocent people who don't deserve to be landed with any more trouble.'

'Irena Vourlamis, for example?' she asked, and saw

his face grow taut again, the blue eyes harden.

'For God's sake . . .' He pushed his plate away and got up. 'Fruit or cheese?' he asked, walking away towards the hob and putting the perculator on to it.

'Fruit would be fine.'

He brought a large wooden bowl of fruit over to the table; removed their two plates and the meat and salad. Nicole chose an orange and began to peel it. Frazer moved back with some fetta cheese and sat down opposite her again.

'I've read your books,' she said. 'I enjoyed them; you're a very good writer, it was like hearing you talk to read them.' She looked at his face, which was polite.

'Thank you.' He got up again and went to make the coffee, brought her a cup. 'Do you want to drink it here or shall we go and listen to some music while we have our coffee?'

'As you prefer.' Nicole was feeling impatient because he had brushed aside what she said about his books; wasn't there any subject she could bring up without him putting up the shutters on her?

He looked down at her, his mouth indented. 'Now what's wrong? You look like a wet Monday.'

'Why are you so secretive? Can't I even say I like your books?'

He ran one finger lightly down the centre of her nose and touched his finger tip to her lips. 'Sorry, I was too pleased to know what to say.' He smiled at her, his eyes a deep gleaming blue in his tanned face, and Nicole smiled back. She got up and they walked into the sitting-room; it was more comfortable now, he had cleared away some of the books and records which had littered every surface. She sat down on a deep, upholstered chair and Frazer went to the stereo unit.

'Any music you prefer? You used to like jazz, didn't you?'

'Still do.'

'Billie Holliday?'

'Fantastic,' she said, and he put on an LP of old hits she knew very well and always enjoyed. He sat down on the floor, his chin propped on his knees and his eyes brooding on her face.

'Can't we call a truce? You're only going to be here for two weeks—we've got a lot of ground to cover, must you keep wasting time on stupid, pointless inquisitions about things that are better forgotten?'

In the background Billie Holliday's dark, velvety voice sang: 'Mean to me, why are you so mean to me?' Nicole smiled while Frazer watched her as though trying to read every flicker of expression on her face.

'Tell me about the book you're just finishing—or don't you like to talk about your work while it's in progress?'

'I'm more interested in you. Tell me what you've been doing in the last eight years, apart from turning into a one-woman army.'

'I've told you—working with Sam.'

'Is that all? There must have been other things in your life.'

'Such as?'

'Men,' he said, and her face smoothed out into blankness. 'Why didn't you marry Bevis?' he asked abruptly, and she stared at him, her mouth parted in puzzled disbelief.

'Bevis?'

'Yes, Bevis,' he said irritably. 'What went wrong? Why didn't you marry him?'

'What *is* this obsession with Bevis? There was nothing between Bevis and me, I only went around with him when Melanie was with us.'

'Melanie told me you were planning to marry him,' he said, and Nicole stiffened, her ears deafened by the over-rapid pulse of her own blood. She stared at him and his brooding, watchful eyes stared back.

'No! I don't believe you,' she protested—but she did believe him, and a blinding white light had lit up the past, making a lot of things very clear.

'She said you were secretly in love with Bevis but Sam didn't approve of him and because you were still so young you had to wait.'

'When did she tell you this?' When had Melanie had a chance to talk to him without being overheard? Nicole couldn't remember Melanie being alone with him.

'In Paris,' he said, and Melanie had told her that she had met Frazer again in Paris—but that had been after Frazer had stood her up on that last date.

'I had to go over there on an urgent story,' he said, his chin on his knees. 'We had a date, I couldn't make it because the paper sent me off without warning. I rang to tell you . . .'

'Rang?' Nicole interrupted sharply, her eyes brilliant with anger.

He nodded. 'You were in the bath or something— Melanie answered, she said she'd give you my message.'

'She didn't,' Nicole said flatly. How could Melanie have done it? She had been dancing about that evening, all smiles; whispering to Bevis behind Nicole's back, busily conspiring, and Nicole hadn't once suspected it.

'Didn't?' Frazer stared but didn't seem surprised, although his brows drew together in a black frown. 'I couldn't wait to talk to you, my flight was being called, I was ringing from Heathrow. I hung up and when I got to Paris a few hours later I rang you from my hotel. Sam said you were out with Bevis.'

'And Melanie,' she said.

Frazer didn't seem to hear that, he went on talking in a low, curt voice. 'I was kept running around for the next couple of days, but I rang you twice—you were out, I suppose, so was Sam; I didn't get through. And then Melanie turned up. She said she was visiting an old friend.' He caught Nicole's eye and grimaced angrily. 'No, I wasn't dumb enough to believe her, but then she told me that I was making life difficult for you and Bevis. Sam was encouraging you to see me, she said. He approved of me, but having me around was a problem, it meant you couldn't see Bevis. She talked so frankly, she was very sympathetic—said you hadn't been able to bring yourself to tell me the truth, you didn't want to hurt me.'

'Oh, my God,' Nicole muttered, putting her hands over her face, shaking with a mixture of anger with Melanie and a dazed rage with herself for not having guessed at the time that Frazer's disappearance was somehow contrived by Melanie. She had been too busy being bitter over Frazer to spare the time to think about Melanie's part in what happened. Even when Melanie told her that she was going to marry Frazer she had instinctively blamed Frazer; she had thought that he had dropped her in order to pursue Melanie.

Frazer was silent for a minute, she felt him watching her, then as she looked up, very pale, he said: 'I think the story gelled for me when she told me how much I'd bothered you when I tried to make love to you.' His voice was incisive, hard. 'I knew that was true; when I touched you that night you leapt like a scalded cat.'

She looked away. Didn't I ever suspect that Melanie had somehow lied to me? she asked herself. I couldn't work out how she'd done it, but I knew—of course I knew. That was why I wouldn't go to the wedding or see her again. I didn't know how she'd managed to do it, but I knew *what* she'd done, my intuition picked it up without my brain ever working it out.

'Melanie was my best friend,' she said huskily, because that was what hurt; she had loved Melanie and Melanie had betrayed her.

'Melanie was her own best friend—she didn't have any others, she didn't need them,' Frazer said savagely.

Nicole turned on him, trembling with pain and rage. 'Okay, she lied to you, but if you'd been determined to find out the truth you'd have asked Sam. You didn't. You accepted what she'd said without so much as trying to check it. I thought you were a good reporter, is that how you got your stories?'

He flushed a dark, angry red. 'I told you the truth was never easy. I've left out a few things.' He paused, his eyes grim. 'Like, for instance, that I slept with her that night.'

Nicole felt a jerk of pain; it was stupid to care, he and Melanie had been married for six years after that, but she *did* care. Her pallor increased, her mouth trembled, then tightened.

Frazer was watching every flicker of expression intently and he looked harsh. 'I sure as hell didn't intend to, but I realised later that she'd intended it. She was getting me into a situation where I was trapped. Once I'd made love to her I couldn't go back to you. I knew that much about you.' He smiled at her bitterly. 'That's true, isn't it? You'd never have forgiven me. I saw your face just now, that's how you would have looked if I'd come and told you I'd been to bed with her in Paris. Whether the story about Bevis was true or not, I had no chance with you.'

'So you married her,' Nicole said flatly.

'I had to—she told me she was pregnant.'

'Oh,' Nicole said, drawing a sharp breath, and he nodded.

'It was a lie, of course, but I didn't discover that until after I'd married her. She invented that story because she knew I didn't want to see her again; she pursued me until I was dizzy, kept turning up at my flat, ringing me at the office.'

'She must have been crazy about you,' said Nicole, hating him and feeling sorry for Melanie faced with his indifference.

'You really don't know much about her at all, do you?' Frazer answered as though he pitied her, and she suddenly couldn't stand any more. She got up, looking at her watch.

'I'm very tired, I think I'll get off to bed.' She walked to the door and he stayed where he was, looking drained and weary. 'Goodnight,' she said, and he answered in a dull voice, 'Goodnight, Nicole.'

She despised herself because she was running away from the truth; she had chickened out because she found it all too painful, she didn't want to hear any more about it—after all, it had been eight years ago, they had all changed beyond recognition and Melanie was dead.

Melanie was dead. When she lied and cheated to get Frazer, she had only been nineteen, and in spite of her outward sophistication she had been a very young nineteen because she had been so spoilt. She had been a sophisticated child; knowing and wilful and without integrity, but a lot of that had not been her fault, it had been the fault of her father who neglected her and had his mistresses openly in their house, the fault of Bevis who drank too much too young, went to wild parties and took Melanie while she was still a schoolgirl, introduced Melanie to drink and probably drugs. Melanie had been the product of genetics and her environment, she had grown up in the belief that you had a right to what you wanted and a right to get it in any way you found necessary. Amoral, uninhibited and without any real idea of what life was all about at nineteen—and dead when she was twenty-five.

Nicole found it all too painful to think about. She turned over on to her face and went to sleep.

When she woke up the sun was already quite hot, and she felt dead and heavy as she showered and got dressed. It was only then that she remembered the photograph album. She was about to get it out from under the mattress when Frazer tapped on the door.

'Want some coffee? I thought I heard you stirring. Are you up and coming down, or would you like it in bed?' There was an ambiguous ring to that question.

'I'm coming down,' she said hurriedly, and made her bed before she left the room. She did not want the cleaner to find the album.

Frazer was in the kitchen drinking coffee at the table with a plate and a half-eaten roll in front of him. 'Sleep well?' he asked, and she nodded, sitting down. She refused the basket of rolls he offered and just had coffee.

He was reading a Greek newspaper, for several minutes neither of them spoke, then he glanced at her over the top of it, one brow moving up.

'You look like someone with a hangover—didn't you sleep?'

'Like a log.'

'Bad dreams?' he asked, and their eyes met in a silent understanding.

'I don't remember.' Had he had bad dreams about Melanie? This morning Nicole still could not find any real hatred for Melanie inside herself; perhaps her death had given her a form of absolution, or perhaps, Nicole thought, she herself was mature enough now to forgive Melanie for what she had done because she could see how Melanie's nature had been formed. The bedrock of Melanie's character had been so sweet; as a little girl she had been very lovable.

'What do you plan to do this morning?' asked Frazer, putting down the paper.

'I thought I'd walk up the hill and look at the windmills.' They stood above Mykonos on the windy slopes facing the sea; white stone windmills with grey cloth sails which flapped endlessly in the face of sea-born gales. They were one of the chief tourist sights; everyone climbed up the hill to walk round them and hear the rattle of the sails.

'I have to work,' said Frazer, getting up and removing his plate. 'My cleaner comes in at ten o'clock; she'll do the washing up.'

Nicole nodded. 'I'll have my lunch in one of the tavernas. If I'm ever in your way you only have to . . .'

'Come and go as you please,' Frazer told her. 'Enjoy your holiday. You'll have dinner with me?'

She hesitated and he smiled at her abruptly. 'Please,' he said, and she nodded.

'Thanks, I'd love to.'

When she left the house ten minutes later, the sun already divided the curving, close-walled streets into a chequerboard of black and white. Nicole moved slowly on the sunny side; cool as yet in her simple yellow cotton dress which was sleeveless and had a low, scooped neckline. As she passed a bearded Greek priest in inky black robes sweeping down to his feet, he turned his head aside in affront at the display of so much of her smooth, tanned flesh.

Nicole paused to look at some straw hats hanging up outside a small shop; she went in to buy a large white one which would protect her nape from the glaring sun. She came out and walked on, wearing the hat, absently noticing the man walking in front of her. It was a minute or two before she realised that it was Paul Vourlamis. He was walking slowly, his head bent, his hands in the pockets of his grey trousers. She couldn't see his face, but she picked up dejection in the way his body moved.

He turned off up a rough path climbing the hill behind the town. It led to the windmills. Nicole followed him, feeling the sudden onslaught of the wind as she moved out of the protection of the narrow streets. She saw Paul Vourlamis's black hair blow around his head, his white shirt ballooning above his belted waist. As he got to the summit he glanced back casually and then she felt his face change; he had recognised her. They had never met, but this was a small place; he would know everyone, and at this time of the season there would be few tourists around. Nicole felt Paul Vourlamis stare fixedly at her, then he turned and hurried away, leaving her with an impression that he was avoiding her.

She reached the top of the path and began to walk to the nearest windmill. Above her the patched sails flapped fiercely and the white mill itself had a dazzling glare in the sunlight. The exposed hills rose bare and stark beyond; dotted with a few new white villas which looked empty; perhaps they were holiday homes for the visiting Americans who came in summer.

Nicole stared out across the blue, glittering sea and the headlands on either side of the bay. The view was breathtaking. She walked round the windmill and came face to face with Paul Vourlamis. Nicole met his black eyes, smiled.

'Hallo, Mr Vourlamis.' She spoke because she was curious to see what his response would be; it might be very enlightening.

He stared at her, then he looked around them. They were quite alone, in the shade of the windmill, out of sight of the town, below. He took an angry stride closer and with his face only inches away from hers hissed: 'Why can't you leave us alone? It was an accident, that was all, an accident. Tell her brother that, tell him to leave us alone!'

Before Nicole could answer he had gone; his long legs taking him out of sight while she stared after him, her mind busy working out what he had said and why he had said it.

CHAPTER EIGHT

SHE walked back into Mykonos, her mind busy with the new thoughts which Paul Vourlamis had handed it. She met Adoni on the waterfront, he seemed to be there all day. The wind had risen suddenly, and moaned and shrieked through the narrow streets as though they were a wind tunnel. Nicole's silvery hair blew around her face and her bare arms were cold, in spite of the sun. Watching her shiver, Adoni asked coaxingly: 'You cold? Want warm shawl?'

Nicole laughed. 'And you know where I could get one, I suppose?' Adoni lived by being a middle-man, leading tourists to shops which paid him commission.

'Very good shawls, very pretty,' he said, his black eyes melting with smiles.

Nicole let him persuade her; she was tempted by the soft white wool shawls anyway. As they walked to the waterfront again, she asked him: 'You knew Kyria Holt?' and watched as he suddenly became blank.

'Ne,' he admitted, lapsing at once into protective Greek.

Nicole had halted at the waterfront taverna where she had eaten the day before; the waiter recognised her and gave her a smiling welcome as she sat down. Adoni said something to the other man who nodded. ''Bye, Nicole,' said Adoni with a hurried smile, and vanished. Wryly she watched him, then glanced at the chalked-up menu and ordered stuffed tomatoes followed by souvlakia, the only meat dish available. Some other tourists arrived and sat down next to her; talking and laughing. They were German, but they seemed to speak some Greek, unlike Nicole who had to consult her phrase book.

Later that afternoon she visited some of the island churches; relieved to escape from the shrieking wind and the brazen sun into the cool, quiet shadow where icons glittered on stone walls and rows of thin yellow candles burnt and smoked. The air was always heavy with incense and the sound of her footsteps rang on marble floors. The icons stared back at her as she stood in front of them; their slanting black eyes remote and filled with a compassionate melancholy as though everything they saw saddened them. She knew how they felt; she stared at them and thought of Melanie stranded here; lost and lonely except when the tourists were here in high summer. Why had Frazer made her stay?

He didn't love her, Nicole thought. She had thought he must have done, but now she knew he hadn't; he didn't talk about Melanie the way a man talks about a woman he has loved. He talked about her with wry understanding, with a sort of tired scorn, but never with anything which held the echo of real emotion.

Melanie had hated Mykonos, but Frazer had made her stay here, although he didn't love her. Why?

Nicole could understand why Frazer loved this island; there was a gay, fierce simplicity about the place with its barren hillsides and white, geometric houses, its flapping windmill sails and howling winds, always battering the little town, making you aware of the sea. Frazer loved to sail, he enjoyed the freedom of the wind, he liked this life; no doubt he went out in the evenings to the brightly lit tavernas where the men sat talking of world affairs with all the excitement of the Greek for politics.

He had chosen to stay here because Mykonos suited him—but why had he made Melanie stay here with him if she had so frantically wanted to get away?

When Nicole got back to Frazer's house the gate was open and the courtyard bathed in a violet light from the sun as it sank down the sky and deepened the twilight shadows. She heard voices inside the house as she opened the door; Greek voices talking in that harsh, rapid way which they used when they were excited; or angry, she thought, pausing in the corridor to listen. Now that she was closer she could distinguish Frazer's voice; he was speaking Greek so fluently she hadn't realised it was him at first. Who was the other man?

The door into Frazer's study was flung open and Paul Vourlamis came out, almost walking into her. He stopped dead, stared at her, his black eyes spitting fury, then walked past her without a word.

Frazer stared at her from the room. 'How long have you been standing there?' he asked.

'What were you quarrelling about?' she fenced. 'Melanie?'

His frown deepened. 'How good is your Greek?'

'Did Paul have an affair with her?' Nicole was guessing, but she saw from Frazer's face that she had hit on the truth; hadn't she already suspected it when Paul Vourlamis spoke to her beside the windmill?

'Was he with her that night? Did they go over to Delos to make love without anyone seeing them? What happened? He said it was an accident—what sort of accident? Did they quarrel?' She threw the questions at him rapidly, watching him.

Frazer ran his hands over his face, his shoulders tense. 'My God, you're like the Spanish Inquisition; don't you ever stop asking questions? Why can't you leave it alone? What good do you think you'll do, raking up the past?'

'I want to know,' said Nicole, and that was the truth. She wanted to know what had happened to Melanie, she needed to know, for so many reasons that she couldn't sort them all out.

Frazer turned and walked away and she went into the room. He threw himself down on to a couch and lay there, his hands over his face. She sat down on a chair and watched him.

'I don't even know where to begin,' said Frazer, letting his hands drop. 'After Melanie and I were married and lived in London? I was working hard, I was angry with her because I'd found out by then that she'd lied when she said she was going to have a baby. She went on going to parties, she saw too much of Bevis, he had a bad influence on her. I started to think he was on drugs . . .'

Nicole drew a sharp breath and Frazer turned his head to stare at her, his mouth twisting. 'Oh, you knew that?'

'I guessed.'

'He's weak and hasn't any self-discipline.' It was easy for Frazer to be so contemptuous; he was a strong man, his hard face told you that discipline came easily to him. 'I asked him point-blank—are you taking drugs? And he laughed and said: who isn't? I'd just sold my first book, my accountant warned me I'd be paying pretty hefty taxes in a year or two if I stayed in England, so I decided to go abroad and take Melanie with me, get her away from Bevis. I didn't realise I was too late, the damage was done.'

Nicole stared at him, her green eyes sombre. 'She was already taking drugs?'

He nodded. 'It took a while to sink in, but then I started trying to persuade her to have help, see doctors. She spent a few months in a clinic and when she came out I thought she was cured. I kept her here because I could watch her, make sure she didn't have access to drugs. She hated it, but her health had improved; she was sleeping better and eating again. Before that she'd lost so much weight, she was a shadow of herself.' He sighed. 'I can't pretend she was happy, she wasn't; but at least she was alive—if she'd gone on living the way she did in London, she wouldn't have lived long. I thought I was doing the right thing; I was trying to protect her.' He sat up, his eyes meeting Nicole's in a direct, grim stare. 'You may not find that easy to believe, but I give you my word of honour. I wasn't being vindictive or cruel. I was sorry for her, she was like a spoilt child, I felt I'd been landed with the responsibility for her and I tried to do my best for her.'

'Without caring for her,' Nicole said in a flat voice.

Frazer grimaced. 'I didn't love her, no. I can't pretend I did.'

'You felt she'd trapped you?'

'I didn't just feel it—she *had* trapped me.' He saw the look in her eyes and went on angrily: 'Don't look at me like that—I didn't treat her badly, I promise you I was as kind to her as I could be without letting her destroy herself with drink and drugs the way her brother was wrecking his own life.'

'You locked her up here and watched her like a

policeman,' Nicole said, aching for Melanie. Wild, wilful and spoilt—yes. But Melanie had been more than that, she had been gay and loving and high-spirited, she had been the very last person in the world to respond to being kept in a cage and watched with cool-eyed indifference by the only man around her. In that situation what would Melanie do? Try to escape? Yearn to get back to Bevis but be too scared of Frazer to try to get away?

'Did you tell her you'd kill her if she ever tried to get away?' she asked, and Frazer looked stunned.

'Of course not!' He paused, frowning. 'I may have said it would kill her if she went back to London, but that wasn't a threat; it was a warning.'

One Melanie had misinterpreted, Nicole thought, or had he phrased it ambiguously? Had it sounded to Melanie like a deadly threat?

He was watching her face intently. 'Nicole, she was never in love with me—if you're imagining that I hurt Melanie in that way, you're very wrong. She wasn't capable of love; I don't know why she pursued me the way she did, but . . .'

'I know why,' Nicole said drily, and he stopped and stared at her.

'Well?' He waited and she thought, looking for a way to phrase it which wouldn't give away too much of her own feelings. Frazer moved impatiently, his blue eyes fierce. 'If you know, out with it; don't sit there being cryptic and mysterious.'

'You ran away,' Nicole said. 'If you'd fallen head over heels for her, she wouldn't have thought twice about you, but you kept being evasive and so Melanie kept trying to get you.' She gave him an ironic smile. 'So you see, I do know Melanie very well. You were wrong about how I saw her. I saw her pretty clearly.' Melanie had been desperate enough to invent a false pregnancy; it had driven her crazy that Frazer wasn't interested in her. She had always got what she wanted; she couldn't bear it when Frazer said no to her.

Frazer gave a short sigh. 'Yes, you're right. Maybe I should have offered her a divorce later, I thought about it, but I was afraid she would go right back to her old life and get hooked on drugs again. I may never have been in love with her, but I felt responsible, you see. I thought I'd wait and see if she changed as she got older; she was so young.'

'When did she start the affair with Paul Vourlamis?' Nicole asked, and Frazer didn't answer, he shook his head at her.

'I'm prepared to tell you everything about myself and Melanie, but I'm not talking about other people. I told you that. You seem to think that someone killed her—I assure you, Melanie destroyed herself; the only help she had was from Bevis, and the saddest part of that is that Bevis loved her. I've never doubted that; he's half crazy now, but he really cared about his sister. That's why I could never tell him what he did to her; if he believed me it would kill him, if he didn't it would be because he couldn't bear to face the truth.'

'Can you?' Nicole asked, and he stared at her, brows furrowed. 'If she stayed with you, isn't it possible she really loved you all the time?'

'No,' Frazer denied curtly. 'Do you think I wouldn't have known?'

'You didn't love her, you've admitted it.'

'I'm sensitive enough to feel someone else's emotions if they're that strong,' he said drily.

'Are you?' She looked at him and Frazer's face changed, his blue eyes darkened and his mouth wasn't quite so steady.

'When we first met you were very young, too—but . . .'

'I don't want to talk about myself!' she said desperately, flushing. He couldn't have failed to see her feelings; she hadn't known how to hide them. 'I was talking about Melanie—hasn't it ever occurred to you that you might be a father figure to her?'

He looked stunned. 'My God, no!'

'Her own father ignored her, you know; I wonder if the hectic way she ran around trying to get attention wasn't a subconscious attempt to get *his* attention? Isn't that how children behave?'

'I've never thought of myself as a father figure before,' he muttered with grim amusement. 'Is that how *you* see me?' He darted her a mocking look, she flushed again and ignored him. 'I suppose it's possible; we'll never know.'

Maybe it was pointless to speculate now, Nicole thought. Had Melanie always been slightly jealous of Sam's devoted affection, though? She had tried to coax Sam into being fond of her at an early stage and failed. Had she tried to get Frazer away from Nicole because Frazer was an authoritative figure; adult and mature and tailor-made to be a godlike father figure?

'You were lucky,' Frazer said suddenly. 'You had a firm background; Sam and your parents had taught you to be self-reliant and self-confident. You had more going for you than Melanie ever did.'

'I used to envy her,' Nicole said. 'She was so pretty and popular; everyone loved her. I was always the odd one out; gawky and selfconscious, I could never make friends quickly the way Melanie did. I thought she was the lucky one, then.'

'You were wrong,' he said.

'Yes. But that's easy to say with hindsight.'

'Why did you come, Nicole?' he asked very quietly. 'What were you trying to find out? Was this some sort of pilgrimage? On your own behalf—or Melanie's?'

'I lied to you. I did see Bevis, he did tell me Melanie was dead.'

Frazer sat upright, staring at her fixedly. She looked down at her hands lying loosely in her lap and twined her fingers together as she told him how she had come to meet Bevis again and what Bevis had told her. This time she told him the exact truth; there was no point in lying any more, she was certain she knew what had happened between him and Melanie, between Melanie and Paul Vourlamis. Frazer hadn't been lying to her just now when he said Melanie destroyed herself—but Bevis had been lying when he told her he believed Frazer had killed his sister. Bevis had hated Frazer, he was a drug addict, which was no doubt why he had been having hassle from those thugs that night. He hadn't wanted the police called because he couldn't afford to get involved with the police; Bevis lived outside the law.

She told Frazer all about that, too, and Frazer said: 'He has to get money for drugs somehow; he's probably mixed up with criminals.'

'That was what I worked out at the time. He was getting a beating up because he'd made someone angry, and he knew those boys. He was more scared of the police than anything else.'

'Did he know you were coming here? Did you tell him you'd come?'

She shook her head.

'You're very discreet,' Frazer drawled, and she smiled up at him, leaning back with her arms raised over her head, linking them above her silvery hair.

'In my job I have to be.'

'I like you better when you're not so cool,' he said softly, and Nicole felt a flicker of panic. She got up and Frazer rose at the same instant, blocking her way as she moved towards the door.

'I'm going to have a shower before dinner,' she said huskily. A strange trembling sensation had begun inside her as Frazer moved closer, his eyes brooding on her face.

'But then that's half your fascination,' he went on, ignoring her remark. 'On the surface you're cool and very together, a tough lady to tangle with—but you said yourself, nobody changes that much; underneath there must still be that girl I met in Mallaig.' He caught her face between his hands before she could move back; his fingertips pressed against her pale temples and he stared down into her eyes. 'Where is she? In here . . .' His fingers were forced down against the bones and she gave a little gasp of protest.

As her mouth parted, Frazer bent and kissed it, and at the first touch of his mouth she felt flame shoot through her body, it arched towards him in an involuntary movement, and his hand dropped to curve round her waist and pull her closer. She weakly lifted her own arms and slid them round his neck, her senses leaping with a powerful desire which wiped out of her mind everything else but the satisfaction her body was demanding.

Eight years ago she had ached to have Frazer make love to her; he had awakened her sensuality without ever satisfying it, and she hadn't allowed anyone to get that close again. She hadn't met anyone who matched up to the masculine image Frazer had imprinted on her imagination all those years ago. She kissed him passionately, trembling as his hands gently touched her, but even now she couldn't silence her mind; it kept pushing questions at her, tormenting her with uncertainties.

She pulled back her head, breathing thickly, and Frazer looked down at her with eyes which leapt with feeling.

'Have you had an affair with Irena Vourlamis?' Nicole stammered huskily.

He swore, closing his eyes briefly. They opened again and the blue depths of them were volcanic with rage. 'No!'

'Then why . . .'

'Nicole,' he interrupted harshly, 'will you for pity's sake stop this? Irena has never so much as looked at anyone but Paul. She'd be staggered if you suggested there'd ever been anything between us.'

'I had to know,' she said, her eyes pleading with him to understand. 'Can't you see that? If you'd been making love to her I had to know.'

'Will you stop acting like a human ferret and start feeling like a woman?' Frazer demanded, staring down at her face. 'Or don't you know how?'

She flushed hotly, then laughed, almost on the point of tears. 'Maybe I've forgotten how . . .'

'Then you need a refresher course,' he said, catching her by the wrist, his fingers biting into her flesh. He walked away, pulling her after him, and Nicole tugged at her imprisoned wrist without being able to unlock his grip.

'Frazer, what do you think you're doing . . . where are we going . . .' Her question died away without needing an answer as he began to climb the stairs, with her in tow, stumbling at the pace he set.

'I'm not going to bed with you,' Nicole said to his back. He ignored her; the only reaction she got was that his fingers bit more deeply into her wrist.

'What do you think I am?' she demanded as he pulled her across the landing towards her bedroom. 'This caveman stuff may go down well with some women, but I prefer to pick my own time and place, and I haven't made up my mind yet.'

He stopped by the bed and let go of her wrist. She stared at him, her mouth dry as she recognised the expression on his face.

'Make it up, then,' Frazer said in a deep, slightly unsteady voice. 'Now.'

'Just like that?' She tried to laugh, but it wasn't very successful; her mouth was trembling too much. She pushed a shaky hand through her ruffled silvery hair, trying to think; her mind was in chaos, she was torn between the insistent demand of her own senses and the quiet, still voice of her wary intelligence.

'Scared?' Frazer taunted, and she couldn't laugh that off because it was far too close to home. She was frightened; frightened of what would happen to her if she let him make love to her, because she wanted him more than she had ever imagined she would ever want anyone or anything and it scared her stupid to contemplate allowing her mind to drown in the mindless intensity she suspected he could unleash in her. Nicole was terrified of her own emotions.

He took a step closer and she flinched. 'Can't you wait . . .' she began, and he shook his head.

'I've waited eight years,' he said, and his hands silkily stroked her bare arms upwards to her shoulders. 'You were like a nervous cat; you shivered when I touched you, but you were only nineteen. You're a woman now, don't tell me you haven't had a little more experience since then.'

'Not much,' she whispered. It was true; she had had dates with men, they had made love to her and she had never felt like this, she felt as though it was the first time a man had ever touched her. In the past it had always been she who controlled the situation; she had never felt her grip on herself threatened, but Frazer was the one controlling her tonight. He might have told her she had to make up her mind, but she knew with a shiver of alarmed recoil that if she let him make love to her she wouldn't be able to control either of them.

Frazer was watching her intently. His hand slipped down from her shoulder to her breast and his head bent, he kissed her neck while his seductive fingers lazily caressed her. 'If you hadn't felt something for me you wouldn't be here,' he whispered against her skin, and she couldn't deny that. She had told herself she had come to Mykonos to find out the truth of what happened to Melanie, and in one sense that was true; but she had also come here because for eight years she had been aching with frustration and Frazer was the one man she had ever wanted with this deep, aching need.

'You're beautiful, I knew you were going to be beautiful one day,' he told her, and found her mouth.

Her hands went up to catch his head; her lips parted and she groaned as the kiss became so passionate it hurt. His hands were moving over her, they seemed to flutter like tormenting moths down her body, their pressure light. She was too intent on her own hungry response to his kiss to realise that he was softly peeling off her clothes until she became aware of the sensuous brush of his fingertips on her bare flesh. His knee nudged her gently backwards, he bent her down until she lay on the bed, shuddering in aroused excitement.

He lay beside her, his body curving into her own, his mouth teasing hers while his hands pursued their private pilgrimage from the warm fullness of her breasts to her thighs. She heard him whispering, his mouth an inch above her own, 'Do you want me, Nicole?'

He was asking the question, but his own voice was answering it, those intrusive hands were answering it— Frazer thought he knew how she felt and of course he was right, how could she hide what her body betrayed to him?

'Did you ever think of me?' she asked, and hadn't even known she needed to know if he had until she heard herself asking.

She heard the rough intake of his breath. He lay still, his face hidden. 'I tried not to,' he said after a moment. 'I thought I'd never see you again. I thought I'd missed my chance, and that hurt like hell. If only you hadn't been so young! I suppose I didn't know how to handle how I felt at the time, I made stupid mistakes. I was ridiculously over-sensitive about you—when you're uncertain you leap to stupid conclusions. That's why Melanie managed to convince me you didn't like me the way I'd hoped you did. I often think women don't realise how baffling they are to men; I was half afraid of you, scared of rushing it and frightening you away. That night I tried to make love to you I knew you hated it . . .'

She laughed, 'Frazer, you idiot!'

He lifted his head. 'Didn't you?'

'Never mind that,' she said quickly, unwilling to admit too much too soon. 'How did Melanie trap you? You said you didn't intend to sleep with her—why did you?'

He sighed harshly. 'I got drunk.'

'Oh,' she said, her mouth wry.

'Yes—when I woke up she was in my bed. I've no idea what happened the night before—but she told me we'd made love, and she'd certainly spent the night with me.'

Had Melanie lied? Nicole thought, and Frazer watched her, his eyes grim. 'Yes, I know what you're thinking. Was it true? Do you think it didn't occur to me later that she'd invented that, too? I don't know, I'll never know. I sometimes used to think that Melanie didn't know the difference between truth and lies. She said whatever seemed to her the right thing to say in a given situation, she said whatever would get her what she wanted. She didn't care about consequences or other people's feelings; she only cared about herself, like a small child yelling for what it wants. For all she knew or cared, she might have been the only person in the world.'

'How did you feel when you found her in your bed?' Nicole asked, frowning.

'Guilty and angry and damned worried,' he admitted. 'She laughed, though. She said I needn't look as if I'd broken every one of the Ten Commandments; she hadn't been a virgin, did I think she was a little girl?' He looked away, his face harsh. 'Then she made it clear she wanted to make love again. I had to lose my temper before she would get up and dress. All I could think about was you. I knew that whether what she'd told me about Bevis was true or not, I'd lost any chance with you. By then I could see that Melanie would tell you I'd slept with her . . .'

'She didn't,' Nicole said. 'Not then—she never mentioned you until she came and told me she was marrying you.'

Frazer stared at her. 'My God . . .' His face was baffled. 'But didn't you wonder why you never heard from me again?'

'What do you think?' The retort flashed out of her with something like savagery and Frazer put both arms around her and rocked her on his body, one hand stroking her hair.

'Darling,' he whispered, kissing her eyes, her cheeks, her mouth. She searched for his lips as they were about to move on to her neck and he rolled on to her, pressing her down into the bed as they kissed heatedly.

The deep-seated throbbing of her body grew more fierce, she began to undo the buttons on his shirt with shaky hands and Frazer slid away from her and pulled off his clothes, his outline shadowy in the deepening twilight. The wind had dropped, the night was hushed and drowsy outside in the town. Nicole stared at him, her heart beating with sickening urgency as he moved back towards her, she felt feverish and at the same time icy cold, as though her own desire was a shock to her.

He knelt above her, his knees gripping her waist, and bent to kiss her coaxingly. 'You're cold,' he said huskily. 'We'll have to do something about that.' The teasing, insidious caress of his hands was already sending heat through her veins; she gripped his wide shoulders to pull him down on her and he laughed huskily. Nicole had stopped using her mind; she was giving her emotions full rein and they were dragging her helplessly into a fathomless abyss of passion. She wound her arms round his cool body, kissing him, feeling the firm muscled thighs moving between her own. His lips softly touched the nipples hardening on her breasts, his hands explored the yielding body underneath him, and she threw back her head, groaning, as expert fingers tantalised and excited her. Her jaws were set in a rigid tension, her back arched, with eyes closed tightly against the draining light she gave herself to the pleasure he was giving her. A tightening spiral of sensual tension broke and hoarse little cries broke from her; when she lay still and breathing unevenly, Frazer kissed her, his hand still warmly between her thighs. Nicole lightly ran her hand down his body and felt his flesh stiffen, heard the gasp he gave.

'I want you,' she murmured, a smile in her voice. 'Now.'

'Not cold any more?' he mocked, but he was breathless.

She looked at him through her lashes, her hands running down the curving indentation of his spine, feeling his warm skin against her own and below that the hardness of bone, the firmness of muscle. Night had fallen, extinguishing the last of the light; she couldn't see his features, only the glitter of his eyes were visible, but she did not need to see him to know what he felt, her hands told her all she needed to know.

'No more games,' she said hoarsely, then gave a deep moan of satisfaction as he sank into her. Their flesh clung, moist and heated, she clutched at his back with both hands, her body arching under him in the fierce tension of desire, and then she heard Frazer's thick gasp, his body went rigid, he stopped moving on her, gripped in the wild convulsions of pleasure.

Nicole lay still as he fell down against her, groaning, his face burrowing into her shoulder.

After a minute he muttered: 'Sorry.'

'So I should think!'

He turned his head. 'Angry?'

She laughed and stroked his tumbled black hair. 'A little frustrated, I admit.'

'I couldn't stop it; I wanted you too much.'

'I hope it isn't a habit of yours,' she teased, and he laughed, she felt the shudder of his body as the laughter deepened.

'Next time,' he promised, kissing her warmly, deeply, and she held his head to kiss him back.

'Next time,' she agreed as he lifted his head, and in spite of the unsatisfied aching inside her she felt wildly, stupidly happy.

He rolled down beside her, his arm flung across her body, and they lay in silence in the darkness, their bodies fitting together as though they had been made to do so. Nicole was deeply aware of his arm lying across her in that possessive, protective gesture; his palm warmly curving round her hip.

'Hungry?' Frazer asked suddenly, and she laughed, as though the question was riotously funny. He leaned up on his elbow to peer down at her. 'What's the joke?'

'I don't know,' she said, and she didn't know why she was laughing; except that she was so happy. 'But I am hungry, now you mention it—in fact, I'm starving. What shall we cook?'

'I'm going to have a shower and get dressed, then we'll

go down and hunt in the larder,' he said, getting off the bed in one smooth movement. He bent and kissed her and then picked up his clothes from the floor. 'Ten minutes,' he said, from the door. 'Don't go to sleep.'

'I'm getting up now,' she said without moving. He went out and she stared towards the door, seeing light flowering along the landing as he switched on his bedroom lamp. I love him, she thought, without surprise or doubt. She had known the night she arrived here and saw him walking along the street below her while she stood at the window in the Hotel Delos and watched him with a strong sense of panic. One glimpse of him and she had felt strung-up, disturbed, alarmingly excited.

All these years love had lain dormant inside her, like a seed in dark ground, frozen and motionless, but still alive and ready to break up through that darkness of the heart to find the sun, when it finally shone.

It had amazed her to listen to Frazer's confession of his own uncertainty and hesitation; she had thought him self-confident and sure of himself, it had never entered her head that he might not be entirely in control of his own feelings.

He hadn't said he loved her, she thought, frowning, then her face cleared; hadn't he said it without using the words? Did he even need to say it? She had felt it the minute she was with him, every time they met; whatever they were saying their eyes, their bodies, their minds were talking underneath the words they said, and what they were talking about had had nothing to do with the sharp question-and-answer session going on in the open. She hadn't been able to help looking at him and he had stared back. Every time he touched her he had tightened the coil of sexual attraction between them, yet even the driving necessity for expression which love always brings had only been a small part of how she felt, and was certain he felt. Love meant far more than that; it was a sense of completion when they were together, and even at nineteen Nicole had felt entirely whole when she was with Frazer.

He appeared in the doorway, lithe and amused in black jeans and a dark blue shirt. 'You lazy creature, I thought you were getting dressed?'

He snapped on the light and she blinked, dazed and half asleep. Frazer was staring across the room at her, she felt ridiculously shy as his eyes moved over her naked body.

'I won't be a minute!' She scrambled off the bed and almost ran towards the shower cubicle in the corner of the room.

'Famous last words. I'll get some wine out of the cellar,' he said as she dived into the cubicle and closed the door.

She showered hurriedly and stepped out a few moments later, a towel anchored around her breasts and covering her to the knees. The room was empty, the door shut. Nicole relaxed, smiling to herself; she was behaving like a teenager with a first boy-friend. She dried herself, dressed in a gauzy Greek blouse which she had bought in the shop where she bought the white shawl, put on clean jeans and sat down in front of the dressing-table to brush her drying hair and do her make-up.

Still feeling nervous, she quietly went downstairs, but before she had reached the kitchen she heard Frazer talking in English from his study. Nicole thought for a moment that he was calling her, then she stopped with a frown, listening.

'There's no need to worry about her, Irena. I promise you, she won't be a problem any more—I've dealt with it.'

CHAPTER NINE

NICOLE's body froze in ice-cold shock, but her mind went on working with the clarity of unexpected pain, numbed by it for the first few moments so that she could think fast and sharply.

He had made love to her with what she had believed to be a real, intense passion. She had only just admitted to herself that she was in love with him, she had been in love with him since she was nineteen and during the years in between his image had never left her subconscious; even when she didn't think of him for weeks on end he had been there, present in her memory, unforgotten. That was why she had come all this way. To lay a ghost, she thought, and had to put a hand over her mouth to stifle the bitter, hysterical gasp of angry laughter which struggled to escape.

'That's right,' Frazer said inside the room. He sounded cool and brisk, like a man who has settled a problem efficiently and is congratulating himself—and he had, hadn't he? She was the problem he had dealt with so cleverly and capably. He had taken her to bed to distract her, keep her otherwise occupied, but it had all been planned, he hadn't meant a damn word he had said.

'Yes, very clever,' he said, and she heard him laughing. Bastard, bastard, she thought, shaking. Who was clever? Him? Oh, yes, he was clever, she hoped he'd rot in hell. Was Irena congratulating him on his cute tactics? Had they planned it together? Her face was redhot now, she put shaking hands to it and felt sick.

The oldest trick in the book—and she had fallen for it hook, line and sinker. What do you do with a woman who won't shut up and is making trouble in all directions? Why, seduce her, of course, that will keep her quiet. She stared at the door, hearing his voice talking intimately, softly, in Greek now. Bastard, she whispered so that the word was almost inaudible. I'll get you for this, you bastard!

She couldn't face him yet, she had to pull herself together. She tiptoed back up the stairs and sat down on her bed. Nobody likes to feel they've been made to look a fool; Nicole wanted blood, she was so angry her teeth were grinding together because if she opened her mouth she knew she'd scream. What had he said to her? 'Stop acting like a human ferret?' Oh, yes—she must have begun to find out too much, got too close to whatever he was hiding, or he wouldn't have had to go to such lengths. 'Start feeling like a woman,' the swine had said after that. She despised herself for being such a pushover, how could she have let him do that to her?

'Nicole? Nicole, what the hell are you doing up there?' His voice made her jump; she sat up stiffly, her nerves jangling. 'Nicole! Are we going to eat or not?'

How in heaven's name was she going to make herself sound normal? She mustn't let him guess that she had found out what a two-faced, two-timing devil he was— he thought he had pulled the wool over her eyes and got away with it and for the moment she was going to have to keep up the pretence. If he thought he was safe he'd relax and gradually stop watching her like a cat at a mousehole—and then she might finally uncover the truth.

She moistened her dry lips, forcing them into a wry semblance of a smile to make her voice sound gay and happy.

'Sorry, I'm on my way,' she called back as lightly as she could.

'So I should hope!' Frazer sounded very cheerful; no doubt he was, he would be reeking of self-satisfaction, and she was going to find it hard to hide her own fury in the face of his triumphant grin.

As she walked to the door she remembered the photograph album. She still hadn't had a chance to inspect it, she must do so later. Frazer would probably try to share her bed tonight; she must plead a headache. Not very original, she thought, her lips wry, but a little acting was called for to get her out of this trap. He might imagine she was safely inside, but he was going to find out he was wrong.

By the time she reached the kitchen and found Frazer beating eggs at the table she was wearing what she profoundly hoped was a happy smile. He looked over his shoulder at her, blue eyes glinting through a sweep of black lashes, intimacy in that quick glance, and she thought again: you bastard!

'Hallo, darling,' she said with melting sweetness, and came over to his side to kiss him on the cheek.

'Don't tempt me, woman, I'm too busy to cope with you right now.' He gestured to a plate lying on the table. 'I thought we'd have Spanish omelette; I've got some peppers and tomatoes and some cold cooked potatoes and bits of boiled bacon.'

'You're the boss,' Nicole said, and gave him a luminous smile, her green eyes misty with what she hoped he would take for passion but which was really a desire to batter his head in with a blunt instrument.

'Very feminine,' Frazer approved, and she held on to her smile with great difficulty. 'Could you mix a salad and make the dressing while I do the omelettes?'

'Salad in the fridge?' she asked, and he nodded, moving to the hob to start cooking his mixed ingredients before he poured in the beaten egg.

'I can see you're a useful man to have around,' she mocked as she carefully washed the salad, then hoped he hadn't picked up the underlying tartness of her tone. She didn't want that razor-sharp mind of his working on why she should be sniping at him.

'A man of many talents,' he said, and smiled round at her briefly. She smiled back, her hair bristling on the back of her neck. He certainly didn't undersell himself, did he? She was glad when he went back to his cooking, unaware that she was eyeing the back of his head with extreme dislike and a yearning wish to have something suitably lethal to aim at him.

'So I've noticed,' she said, thinking of the coaxing, expert, damnable hands which had given her such pleasure not long ago. Maybe Frazer picked up some echo in that, because she heard him laugh, a deep warm chuckle.

'The night's young yet,' he said with husky mockery, and she knew he was thinking ahead to when they went back up the stairs to bed, her teeth ground together and she shredded lettuce with venom into the salad bowl. That's what he thought—he wasn't getting *her* back into bed tonight!

'Warm plate, warm plate,' he muttered, pouring eggs

into the delicious mixture cooking in the pan. 'Two minutes, Nicole—is the dressing ready?'

They were working together smoothly; in any other circumstances it could have been such fun. If she hadn't overheard him talking to Irena she would have been walking on air right now and going crazy waiting to make love with him again. How else had he deceived her? she wondered, tossing the salad in the dressing. How much of what he had already told her had been true? How could she ever believe him again? He had neatly led her into this trap and she had blithely been so sure she would be able to avoid the manipulation she had not been so dumb she hadn't anticipated. He had shown her the cheese and the trap and she had flattered herself she wouldn't get caught; she would snatch the cheese and escape. It was maddening to have guessed in advance that Frazer would try to stop her finding out the truth about Melanie by any methods he had to use—and yet to let him hoodwink her just the same.

He had looked her straight in the eyes and said with such convincing anger: 'No!' Of course he wasn't having an affair with Irena Vourlamis, how could Nicole imply such a thing?

What *was* going on between them, anyway? How much of the story he had told her about his marriage to Melanie had been true?

'Ready?' he asked, turning with the two omelettes neatly arranged on warmed plates, and she summoned a brilliant, false smile.

'They look delicious.' They did; he was obviously a good cook.

He poured her some wine and helped himself to some of the salad; a twisty red candle burnt between them, the flame giving off soft blueish wisps of smoke as it flickered in the draught from the window. Moths flapped against the glass and left powdery glistening smudges where their wings brushed it. Nicole forked omelette into her mouth and felt languid and sleepy; anger was tiring.

'That's the fourth yawn in five minutes,' Frazer remarked, and she looked at him, trying to stifle the next yawn.

'Sorry, I must be tired.'

'Worn out, are you?' he mocked with enjoyment as a slight flush rose in her cheeks.

'I must be, it's the sea air.'

'Oh, is that what it is?'

She laughed, hiding her resentment. He was determined to have his fun, let him; if he could act his head off, so could she.

'I'm having trouble keeping awake,' she said. 'In spite of this gorgeous food—where did you learn to make omelettes as good as this?'

'Spain, where else?' He talked about a trip he had made there a year ago, to do publicity for his latest book, and she listened with drooping eyelids, careful to let him notice.

She cleared the table later while he got the coffee, but she only sipped at her cup, and after a time Frazer smiled at her with what might have been a totally convincing display of tenderness if she hadn't known better.

'Look, why don't you get off to bed? I'll wash up. You look as if you're dead on your feet.'

She pretended to hesitate. 'But . . . you won't mind? I mean . . .'

He knew what she meant and he laughed softly, taking her cup away and kissing her mouth with lingering warmth.

'That can wait, we'll have all the time in the world tomorrow. My cleaner only works in the morning; when she has gone we'll have the house to ourselves.'

'Good,' she said, letting her arms go round his neck. She linked her hands in his hair, suppressing a desire to pull it hard, and kissed him, 'Goodnight, then, see you in the morning.'

All the way up the stairs she was shaking with bitter anger. He was so damned convincing, she had found it hard to believe that his tender amusement was phoney. He was a great loss to the stage, he would have been a natural actor.

When she was back in bed she found that her pretence of being sleepy had become the truth; no sooner was the light out than she felt herself drifting heavily into the shadowy borders of dream and half-waking consciousness. Her tired mind was trying to make sense of all that had happened to her today; all that she had learnt about the past and what she suspected about the present. It was a confused and confusing jumble; her subconscious made strange work of it. Melanie at a party, laughing, while she and Frazer stood in a crowded room and looked at each other and talked in low voices; Nicole felt a piercing intensity of desire as he brushed his fingers against her hand in a secret caress, and then Irena Vourlamis was there and Frazer was talking to her while Nicole watched them and felt so unhappy that she had to turn away. The dream kept changing; backgrounds and people came and went with bewildering rapidity, and once she believed she was awake. She sat up in the bed

thinking: the photograph album, I forgot the photograph album. Then she was dreaming again and twisting
in the tumbled bed with restless uneasiness.

She woke up in a gold and rose morning; the room was
full of light and the sound of birds in the mulberry tree in
the courtyard. Frazer was sitting on her bed, she realised
that he had shaken her. He held out a cup of coffee,
smiling.

'You're a restless sleeper; what a mess you've made of
this bed!'

She sat up to take the cup and he looked at her with
eyes that smouldered, dark blue as midnight, travelling
slowly over the smooth perfect curve of her bare shoulder down over the half-exposed roundness of her breasts
which her movement as she leaned forward had brought
into his view.

'Did I tell you you were beautiful?'

'Yes,' she said, and was angry with herself because the
breathless confusion in her voice was real.

'I wish I didn't have to work today,' he muttered, still
looking at the warm cleft, where a faint shadow lay
between her golden-skinned breasts. Bending forward,
he touched his lips there. 'You smell of roses,' he
whispered against her flesh. His tongue flicked softly and
he whispered: 'You taste of them, too.'

'How *do* roses taste?' she asked with a shudder running through her.

He laughed, the sound half smothered on her skin as
his mouth explored deeper sending icy trickles of a
pleasure close to pain along her spine.

'Don't you know the poem: gather ye rosebuds while
ye may?'

'I hope you haven't forgotten that roses have thorns?'

She pushed his head away because she was enjoying what he was doing far too much.

He sat up, running a hand over his ruffled black hair, and Nicole watched the morning light gleam on his brown skin and the muscular tension of his throat. Her mouth was dry; she recognised the symptom with impatience at her own stupidity. She wanted him. Why pretend she didn't? Her skin was heated and tingling where his lips had grazed it, she hadn't wanted him to stop touching her, she was aching to touch him. She had never felt like this about any man before; the primitive unreachable throb of desire inside her was driving her crazy.

'I just had an agitated phone call from my publisher; he wants my manuscript as soon as I can finish it; I'm up against a deadline. I'm sorry, Nicole—could you find something to do today while I'm working? I should have polished it off by this evening and then I'll be free of all responsibilities.' He grinned at her, getting up with a lazy, graceful movement she watched intently.

'I'll probably sail over to Delos,' she said, and Frazer frowned, his smile vanishing.

'Why Delos? The site's closed today, I think, why not leave Delos until I can come with you and show you round? I know it like the back of my hand.'

Her eyes innocent, she said: 'Okay, that's a deal. Maybe I'll just sunbathe this morning and sail around Mykonos in the afternoon.'

Frazer's frown smoothed out. 'You'll enjoy that; some of the beaches are very beautiful and inaccessible from the land. Have you got a chart? I'll look out mine.'

'Thanks, that would be a help; your charts are probably marked in more detail than mine.'

He got up, but he was still looking at her with a fixed and urgent gaze which was bewilderingly deceptive; she would have sworn it was genuine, just as she could so easily have believed the unsteadiness of his voice as he said: 'My God, I want to get into that bed,' and then laughed roughly. 'But you know that, you wanton, sitting there with that inviting look in your eyes . . .'

Inviting? she thought. Inviting? Is that what it looks like? The only invitation you'll ever get from me is one to jump off the nearest cliff, and you won't have to jump— I'll push you.'

What she actually said was: 'Darling . . .' in tones like melting honey, what she actually did was lie back with her hands linked behind her head and the warm curves of her body in the semi-transparent silk nightdress stretching with sensual awareness while he watched her and breathed audibly.

'Breakfast,' he said with a slur on the word as though he had difficulty getting it out.

'In five minutes,' she promised.

'Five?' He looked disbelieving. 'Be down in ten and I'll be surprised.' He walked to the door, paused there to look back at her, and she hurriedly snatched her alluring smile back from where it had vanished to, her green eyes wide and glowing.

'If you don't want me to come and join you in that bed get out of it and get ready,' Frazer said with teasing laughter, then he was gone and Nicole threw her pillow at the door, soundlessly muttering curses after it.

She got up, then, showered and dressed in white jeans and a white t-shirt which dived down to the cleft of her breasts and left all of her arms and most of her shoulders bare. She brushed her hair, lightly applied pink lipstick to her mouth and went downstairs to find Frazer reading his morning Greek newspaper, the radio quietly playing Greek music and the sunlight picking out blue and silver flashes in his thick black hair.

He looked round, glanced at his watch. 'A miracle! Only seven minutes!'

She joined him at the table, retaining her smile by a struggle of will-power against feeling, poured herself coffee and helped herself to an orange. Frazer watched her deftly peel it.

He started to talk about the morning news from Athens, read her passages from the paper, translating them without hesitation. Nicole ate her orange, drank her coffee and listened while under the cover of her smile her mind was murderous.

He shot a look at his watch, groaned. 'I must get to work. Come into the study and I'll give you the chart.'

She cleared the table, washed her hands and dried them, then followed him into his study. He began to rummage among a pile of charts in a cupboard.

'I know these waters like the back of my hand now, I never use my chart,' he said without looking at her, then exclaimed: 'Ah, here it is . . .'

Nicole took it and smiled tightly. 'Thanks, I'll make sure I let you have it back.'

He put his arms round her waist and she felt his chin on her hair. 'I'll see you later, then,' he said, and again his voice was unsteady. He kissed her eyes and then her mouth, his lips warm and lingering. 'You'd better go or I'll never get to work,' he said as his head lifted, and she hoped the passive yielding of her mouth hadn't made him suspicious. She smiled at him and walked away, feeling the taste of him on her lips, and wondering if she would be haunted by the taste of Frazer Holt for the rest of her life.

'Take care,' he said.

'I will.'

'I wouldn't want to lose you.'

'You won't.' Lose me? she thought bitterly, you're going to wish you'd never seen me, and that's exactly how I feel about you. Loving and hating, walking the dark edge of emotions which cut into you like razors, how could anyone bear such extremity of feeling? She had thought when she was nineteen that Frazer Holt had hurt her so much that she would never know such pain again; she would see to that. She had grown a hard shell of self-sufficiency and cool indifference to everything but her tested affection for Sam and her passion for her job, and it had seemed to work, she had been content enough during these years. Why had she been such a fool as to come looking for Frazer Holt after what he had done to her last time?

She went down to the quayside and the fishermen talking as they mended nets, the boys hanging around watching girls walk by, stared after her and whistled and grinned, but Nicole pretended not to notice any of them. She was in no mood to talk to anyone.

She needed to get away by herself, to be out on the blue water with the wind filling the sails and tossing her hair around her face.

'Hey! Nicole!'

She was just moving away from the quay when the voice alerted her. Looking back, she saw William Old-field, gesticulating, his brown hair whipped back from his forehead and his shirt flapping in the wind.

'Aren't you coming this afternoon?' he bellowed, and she waved and nodded.

'See you later,' she called, her hands cupping around her mouth.

'Midday!' William yelled back, and she saw all the men on the waterfront staring and listening. William turned away and Nicole watched as the men quickly became blank, looking away. She stared back across the widening gap of blue water, noticing that nobody said hallo to William, nor did he seem aware of them. He walked past and might have been invisible. Why didn't anybody on Mykonos like him? But the answer to that was pretty obvious—people like you when you like them, and William didn't care twopence for anyone but himself, he was full of complaints and self-pity. He was living here but hadn't made any friends that she could see; his Greek was limited and ungracious and his manner was offhand.

She turned her back on the island and headed east along the coastline with Delos hidden in pearl and turquoise mist on her right and behind that tiny island the larger one of Rhenia; she got a glimpse of them both some time later as the mist drifted and land loomed through it.

An hour later the weather was clear and brilliantly sunny; the water danced and glittered in fragments of light, almost blinding her as she kept her course, with the barren, rocky hillsides of Mykonos rising high above to meet the vivid blue of the sky.

She thought about Melanie and Irena Vourlamis and her husband and Frazer—she still hadn't worked out the tangled skeins of their relationships, how could she when none of them would tell her the truth? If Frazer had been lying to her consistently how much reliance could she place on what she had learnt from him? Very little. Which brought her back to where she had been when she first arrived; except that now she had more scattered pieces to fit into her jigsaw and none of them seemed to fit; she couldn't make sense of any of it.

Melanie came and went like land hidden in drifting mist; Nicole kept thinking she saw her clearly and then she would be gone again only to reappear on the horizon, mysterious, ambiguous, puzzling.

Or was it Frazer who was the key to this puzzle? His explanation of how he had come to marry Melanie seemed far too glib; would a man like that be tricked into a marriage he did not want? Why should he have accepted Melanie's word for it that Nicole was secretly in love with Bevis? When he told her, he had plausibly explained that he hadn't been thinking clearly, the way he felt had made him swallow Melanie's lies, his own uncertainty had made what Melanie said seem possible.

Uncertainty? Nicole laughed angrily, glaring at a gull winging down from a cliff which soared high above the foam-topped sea that crashed into its base.

Frazer Holt had never been uncertain about anything in his life! Even then, eight years ago, he had been aggressively self-confident, very much in command of himself and anyone else he happened to find littering his path.

Glancing at her watch, she turned back towards the port and saw in the distance a white shape lurking like a shadow on the thin line marking the horizon. The cruise ships would start appearing soon; maybe that one was headed for Mykonos? The spring was in full swing, the season had begun, tourists would throng the narrow streets and pour into the little shops and the tavernas.

When she was back on land she walked to the nearest taverna to have a coffee. While she was slowly sipping it, Irena Vourlamis walked past with a basket on her arm. Her eyes met Nicole's, she smiled, and Nicole was startled by the apparently genuine warmth in her face into smiling back.

Irena halted. 'Frazer finishes his book today?'

Nicole nodded. She looked at the other woman's shopping basket. 'Doing the family shopping?'

It was polite small talk, but she sensed Irena's relief in her casual manner. The other woman's friendly smile widened.

'My husband cannot stand to eat fish after he has been handling them for days on end! He told me: get lamb, get veal, but don't show me any fish!' She laughed and Nicole laughed, the sunlight half blinding her as she looked up at Irena.

'You are going to eat here?' Irena glanced at the chalked menu.

Nicole shook her head. 'I just used the lavatory and now I'm having a coffee while I wait for William Oldfield, he's taking me to Delos.' She told Irena that deliberately, watching her with intent eyes.

'Delos?' said Irena, visibly stiffening. Nicole felt the thrill of the fisherman when his line tightens and he knows there is a fish on the end of it.

'That's right; I'm sure I'll find it very interesting, don't you think so?'

Irena stared at her, transfixed, and Nicole smiled drily.

'I must go,' Irena said with husky unsteadiness, and hurried away. Nicole finished her coffee a few moments before William arrived. As soon as she saw his thin figure, in old blue shorts made out of cut-down jeans, and a blue t-shirt, she stood up, put some coins on the table and walked to meet him.

'Got a lifejacket?' William asked as they made their way towards his boat.

'I left it in my own boat—hang on, I'll fetch it,' she said, and when she got back to him was just lacing the orange lifejacket. She watched William critically as they sailed out of the harbour; he was a competent enough sailor, but as he clambered about he was frowning in that petulant way and swearing under his breath whenever he had to dive out of reach of the swinging beam. He didn't enjoy his sailing, he clearly didn't get the same thrill from fighting the elements as Nicole did. Or Frazer, she thought, and frowned. She didn't want to think about him any more.

'Won't take us half an hour to get there,' said William, beating for Delos with a stiff wind behind them. 'I've brought some food; I know a few sunny spots out of the wind where we can picnic. Delos is even more windy than Mykonos and there's very little shelter.'

The island looked like a tiny green and brown speck in the sea at first, but the speck grew larger as they came closer. Nicole watched it; you could probably walk from one end to the other of it in half an hour, she thought; it was amazingly small when you remembered how powerful it had been during the centuries of Greek power in the classical age. It was baffling that such a tiny island could have become a great commercial centre, until you remembered that it had first been a great religious centre; the most important shrine of Apollo, the god of light and reason, of music and philosophy.

'Apollo was supposed to have been born there, of course,' said William, breaking into her thoughts. 'They've replanted a palm tree on what they think was the spot where he was born; his mother, Leto, was supposed to have given birth under a palm tree. There was one there for centuries; the sacred palm tree, pilgrims used to lay gifts under it.'

Around the base of sheer cliffs Nicole saw nothing but sea breaking, there were no beaches, she thought. How had Melanie drowned from one?

'There's the bay of Phournia,' said William, pointing suddenly. 'That's where your friend's clothes were found.'

Nicole leaned on the side, the creaming wake washing behind her, and stared at the minute stretch of sand; hardly big enough to call a beach, and now that she actually saw it she realised she had been crazy to imagine she would find out anything from seeing it. What could it tell her? Rocks and a strip of pale sand and blue, blue water beyond them. What on earth had Melanie been doing here alone at night?

Had she been alone? If not, who had been with her? Delos wouldn't tell her that, it wouldn't tell her anything; in the sunlight it had an ambivalent, secretive smile that hid what it knew.

They landed on the tiny jetty and walked a few yards to the entrace of the site. William carried a wicker basket over his arm, the food it held covered by a red-checked cloth. He paid the entrance fee and the man at the gate handed him two green tickets.

They walked through the gate and stood staring across

the flat, empty, windy island. The grass was still green at this season, covering the dry ground in whispering waves, but in two or three months it would be parched and yellow. Mount Cynthus climbed up behind the flat plain on the edge of Nicole's vision and in the foreground she saw white stone shimmering through grass and ruined walls gleaming in sunlight. The sun was hot but the wind blew fiercely, keeping the temperature down.

Nicole felt a frisson of poignant awareness at the back of her neck. This was the last place Melanie had ever seen—the thought haunted her. The place had a timeless, atavistic air; it was and had been the home of a god, it was easy to believe that standing here in the sunlight with endless fathoms of blue air arching above you so that however hard you stared your eye drowned in an unimaginable horizon.

She couldn't imagine Delos when the walls stood upright, roofed and full of people, instead of lying like broken teeth among the grass.

'We'll take a look at the temple first, shall we?' William asked. He seemed pleased with himself; he was enjoying playing guide, demonstrating his knowledge of the site. Nicole followed at his heels, staring around her with fascination.

'That's the Agora,' he told her, pointing. 'Over there you have the ruins of houses and shops and workshops—a lot of people lived here in those days; it must have been like an ants' nest, the streets are so narrow you can almost touch the houses on each side. It was a very regimented society; very commercial and very rich, but some of their laws were meant to make you remember that it was a holy place. People weren't allowed to die here, they couldn't be buried, they had to leave the island if they were thought to be dying. When a woman was about to give birth she had to go over to Mykonos or Rhenia; if she was delivered before her time she had to undergo purification. That was because Delos was Apollo's birthplace—no other child must ever be born here, and death was an offence to him, too.'

It's an offence to all of us, Nicole thought, shivering; the ending of something like the beginning, was separate, painfully memorable, oddly melancholy. Between birth and death life lay in sprawled, disparate confusion. How strange that Melanie should come here to die, to the place where death was forbidden, where sharp, white light bathed everything you saw and gave it an undying intensity; so clear, so hard a reality of line and colour.

Delos was open and exposed, air and light all round you, no shade, no trees except for the sacred palm tree rising out of the dried, reedy mosquito-haunted swamp which had once been a sacred lake. There was a quality about the light which made past and future meaningless, only the here and now given meaning as you stood there, alive in the sun, alone with the stone heads of gods and men left dreaming in the grass and littered around them a disorder of white stone blocks, fragments of statues, truncated columns with vivid green lizards running over them, their skins pulsing, pausing to drink in the sunshine before darting away.

'These are the famous lions of Delos,' William said as they walked down a broken pavement beside the archaic white stone statues poised to leap, it seemed, but for ever motionless on their brick plinths. Behind them a little way off rose several columns, all that remained of some ruined temple. While they were looking at the lions and William was continuing with his lecture the sky darkened, the wind became colder and the sun went behind clouds.

'Going to rain,' he said irritably, looking up. 'What a nuisance, I was just going to suggest we had our picnic now—I'm starving.'

'I hope it doesn't rain; we'll get soaked, there isn't any shelter here, is there?' Nicole looked around and saw nowhere to go but the ruined little houses, roofless and open to the wind and weather.

'It's only a shower, it will pass,' William said optimistically as the first heavy drops hit the pavement, leaving dark splashes on white stone.

They dashed through the site, avoiding the fragments littering their path, and stood close together in the lee of a walled house open to the sky.

'It will blow over soon,' said William, and a moment later the sun came out and the rain stopped as suddenly as it had begun. 'Let's eat our lunch now,' he suggested, stepping out of the house. They found a quiet corner of the site and sat on great stone blocks with the checked cloth spread between them and on it laid bread and fruit and cheese, honey cakes and some figs, dried but very sweet. William had bought a bottle of water and two cups. Nicole would have enjoyed herself if he hadn't insisted on going on with his lecture in between each mouthful.

Her attention wandered to a butterfly flittering from a patch of small pink flowers to a clump of asphodel, white and ghostly even in the sunlight; from there to a tiny bright green lizard pretending to be made of stone as he clung to a column, his throat gulping and his round eye watching for insects. Nicole felt drowsy, peaceful; there was no other human being in sight, they were alone in that airy sunlight and William's droning voice reminded her of a bee buzzing in a closed room.

A pebble clattered down the rocky, grey and green slopes of Mount Cynthus and she looked up, startled. William looked up, too. A young man was walking down towards them; he waved and William waved back without visible enthusiasm.

'Who's that?' asked Nicole, and William's mouth took that familiar downward turn, telling her he was offended again, although she couldn't for the life of her work out what had offended him. Was it the newcomer? Was he another of William's enemies? He seemed to have so many; he had spent a lot of time during this trip on filling her in with the minor details of terrible injuries inflicted on him by people she had never met. It had all seemed very petty to Nicole; letters unanswered, looks interpreted as malicious, overheard remarks which sounded to her perfectly innocent. William's mind was as excitable and likely to attack before it is attacked as a scorpion in a glass bottle.

Now he shrugged, muttering: 'One of the site team working here—he's allegedly an archaeologist.'

'Allegedly?' queried Nicole, her finely shaped brows lifting in dry amusement.

'He doesn't seem very good at his job; I showed him something I'd found which was quite definitely fifth century and he told me it was much later, probably Roman. Bloody nerve, I'm making a special study of . . .'

'What's his name?' Nicole asked, interrupting the flow and William sulkily looked at her, his mouth a comically exaggerated downward curve.

'I don't know—ask him.' It was a petulant snap.

'Okay,' said Nicole, getting up.

'Aren't you going to help me clear up?' William asked crossly.

'In a minute; finish your orange.'

Nicole walked away through a litter of stone fragments and thick tangled grass through which she saw wild flowers growing in gay profusion; the island was full of spring flowers, from the tiny yellow stars of celandine to the trembling blood-red petals of anemone. Glancing back, she saw William eating his orange; his very shape full of brooding self-pity. She felt a great surge of relief in getting away from him for a while, sitting listening to him she had got the feeling she was carrying a great weight on her back, like a man staggering along with a grand piano. William had seemed pleasant when she met him first; after a few hours of his company she knew why people on Mykonos avoided him, it was in self-protection. William—to put it brutally—was a drag.

Rounding a broken column she found the young man she had been tracking. He was in a ruined house and apparently measuring the walls, having weighted down one end of his tape-measure with a small stone he was walking to the other corner pulling the tape-measure behind him. Nicole watched him scribble something in a notebook which he then thrust back into the pocket of his jeans.

'Planning to redecorate?' she enquired, and he looked round in surprise, then laughed.

'That's right—what do you think? Some mosaic? Or wallpaper?'

Nicole held out her hand. 'I'm Nicole Lawton—you're an archaeologist, I'm told.'

He came and shook hands. 'I'm Georgi Vourlamis—yes, I'm a . . .' He stopped as she drew an audibly shaken breath, staring at her. 'What's the matter?'

She studied him intently, incredulously. He was in his late twenties, slim and agile with narrow hips and a thin chest, his hair and eyes black, his skin sallow. He was attractive in a slightly melancholy way, but by no means handsome.

'I think I know your brother,' she said slowly. He had to be a relative of Paul Vourlamis, although they didn't look alike.

He stared, smiling, unsurprised. 'Paul? Yes, did Oldfield introduce you?' He had a strangely American twang to his English, she wondered if he had spent some time over there.

'Frazer Holt . . .' she began, and his face lit up in a charming smiled.

'Frazer! You know Frazer, too? Are you living on Mykonos? How long have you been there? I haven't been over for a couple of weeks, I've been too busy settling back in here; we lay off during the winter months, of course, this isn't a very hospitable island in the winter, the winds blow for twenty-four hours a day half the time. So we clear off in the winter and come back in spring.' He looked at her curiously. 'What are you doing on Mykonos? How is Paul? He's back, is he? He was off fishing when I left, did he have a good trip? Plenty of fish?'

'Irena said he was sick of the sight of fish, so I suppose he must have had a good trip.'

He laughed. 'When he gets back he stinks of it, they all do; you get used to the smell. How are the children and Irena? All okay?'

'As far as I know. They're very nice children, aren't they? You're not married?'

His dark eyes smiled: 'I shall be soon—in May. We've had to wait three years; she is in Athens at university, her family wouldn't let us get married until she had got her degree—they gave up so much to give her a good education, you know. Maria feels she owes them. They aren't rich; it was a struggle for them, but she's clever, going to be a lawyer. Next year, when we're married, we're going to the States and I'll get a job there while she does some post-graduate work; she's got a good brain.'

'You must miss her,' Nicole said, her mind working rapidly, adding two and two together and wondering if they came to a neat four.

'Oh, sure,' he said in that American twang. 'It can be lonely here, but I like my work, I keep busy.' He smiled at her wryly. 'Now you know all about me—tell me about yourself—what are you doing here, are you working, a writer? A travel guide?' He studied her, his head on one side. 'I can't guess, you could be anything. You'd better tell me, what are you doing on Mykonos?'

'Visiting me,' said a voice from behind her, and she stiffened before she turned, knowing who she would see and even guessing that behind the casual smile she would find Frazer's eyes as hard as flint and as cold as ice.

CHAPTER TEN

'FRAZER, where on earth did you spring from?' Georgi Vourlamis shook hands with him vigorously, clapping his shoulder with the other hand and laughing. 'I didn't even see you on the site and I was up on the camp working, I should have seen you from up there.'

'I only just got here,' Frazer said with a grim note underlying his tone. Nicole felt him looking at her and didn't meet his eyes. Georgi talked on happily.

'Was that your boat? I saw one heading this way but didn't take much notice; this is good, I was just asking . . .' He stopped and looked at her, his hands spread in a very Greek gesture. 'I forgot your name—sorry.'

'Nicole,' Frazer said tersely as if the name tasted bitter.

'Nicole—of course,' said Georgi, smiling at her. 'I was just asking Nicole about Paul and Irena—everything well?'

'Everything fine,' Frazer said.

They heard a plaintive voice calling from somewhere on the site. 'Nicole . . . Nicole . . . where are you?'

'Oldfield,' Frazer said dispassionately.

'I'd better go,' said Nicole. She smiled at Georgi. 'Nice to have met you, I hope we meet again some time.'

'So do I,' he said, smiling back.

She carefully didn't look at Frazer as she walked out into the sunshine and the blustering wind. William was wandering around with his basket on his arm and a morose look on his face. When he saw her he distinctly pouted; she had to bite her lip not to laugh.

'Where have you been? I've been looking everywhere for you.'

'Sorry, I was talking to . . .'

'You might have waited for me,' William accused. 'I had to collect up all the scraps myself; you can't leave anything on a site like this, you know, this isn't Brighton beach. This is an ancient site and I don't think you're taking it very seriously. Why did you want to come if you weren't going to take an interest in what you were told?'

'The wind is colder,' Nicole said, rubbing her bare arms. 'Maybe we ought to get back to Mykonos before the weather turns nasty again?'

'We haven't seen half there is to see!'

'I think I've seen all I want to see,' Nicole told him ruthlessly. She wanted to get away before Frazer caught up with her; she wasn't going to have a row with him in front of William, and if that meant that William was going to complain and sulk all the way back to Mykonos that was too bad.

She began to walk back through the site with William muttering and growling at her heels; she gathered that she was rapidly joining the ranks of those who had offended William and would never be forgiven, but Nicole couldn't feel disturbed by that prospect. She had realised by now that she would merely be one of the vast majority.

They left through the same gate by which they had entered the site; Nicole resisted the temptation to buy some of the postcards displayed in the kiosk beside it, although William urged her to do so. She hustled him along the narrow concrete jetty in what William obviously felt to be a very undignified manner.

'There's no hurry, the weather isn't that bad,' he muttered as she dropped down into his boat, and he took so long in joining her that she got irritated and told him frankly why she wanted to leave.

'Frazer's here.'

William stared at her. 'So what?' he asked, then went a funny shade of green, gulping in his throat in a way that reminded her of the lizards on the white stone whom she had been watching earlier. 'Will he mind you being with me? Is he . . . are you . . .' He stopped, visibly searching for a polite way of asking what was perfectly obvious, so Nicole helped him out bluntly.

'We're sleeping together, yes, and if he catches us here he may belt you.'

William almost fell over in his haste to cast off, Nicole helped him and wished he would let her do the work without his stumbling, clumsy aid. He just got in her way, and if he hadn't been so slow they would have been away before Frazer raced down the jetty towards them. William saw him coming and made agitated noises as he rushed around.

Frazer leapt down into the boat as Nicole equally quickly leapt to the far side of it, away from his long arm. William stayed out of the way, nervous and shrinking, watching without attempting to intervene.

'Get off,' Frazer muttered through his teeth, grabbing Nicole's arm.

'Get off yourself!' She wrenched herself free and her body tensed as she brought her hand down in a blow that never connected.

'Oh, no, you don't!' Frazer swerved out of reach and

at the same time slid behind her. Remembering what happened last time he got her into that position, she swung to face him; he wasn't tricking her into that hold again. The next second Frazer had lowered his head and butted her in the midriff. She gasped and heard William gasp, too; a peculiar little sound midway between horror and glee.

Frazer hadn't hurt her, merely winded her for a second, but during that brief space of time while she was off balance he grabbed her legs behind the knee and hoisted her, struggling, over his shoulder in a fireman's lift.

'Put me down, you bastard!' Nicole yelled.

'Well, really,' William said happily, shocked either by her language or Frazer's tactics.

Frazer slapped her bottom as he stepped back on to the jetty with her and she squirmed in fury, her face red and her eyes spitting fire.

'I'll kill you,' she promised.

'Probably,' he agreed, walking to his own boat with her.

'Don't think for a minute that you're going to get away with this!'

'Shut up,' he said, dropping her into the bottom of his boat so suddenly that she sprawled, wincing, and took a minute to recover enough to get back on to her feet. As she came upright she saw William's boat moving away! he was staring at them, open-mouthed, but he was making sure he put a safe distance between himself and Frazer.

Frazer gave her a look which held hard mockery. 'Your escort just left.'

'Rat,' Nicole muttered, realising that the only way

she was going to get back to Mykonos now was with Frazer.

'You should know, being a female of the species,' Frazer informed her, getting ready to leave himself.

Nicole sat down, wincing again; her bottom was still sore from making such violent contact with the deck a moment ago.

'I came here to find out what happened to Melanie and before I leave I'm going to know the truth,' she told his back, as she steered for Mykonos.

They drifted out, the wind roaring through the white sails, making them rattle and flap so loudly it was hard to hear yourself speak. Spray blew into her eyes, her hair flew wildly in all directions, half blinding her as it whipped across her face.

'The weather's turning,' said Frazer, standing poised by the mast and looking at the cloudy sky. 'We're in for a storm tonight, I think.'

'We're in for a storm right now,' Nicole assured him, and he ducked as the boom swung.

'Keep her steady,' he bit out, as the wind tried to take the boat and blow her out towards Rhenia.

A few moments later they were both too busy to talk as they fought to stay on course for Mykonos, tacking to avoid the wind which wanted to blow them right off course. They had to zig-zag across the choppy water and it took much longer to reach harbour than it would normally do. They worked deftly and smoothly together as if they could read each other's minds and they did not talk except to yell warnings to each other when it was necessary.

William was ahead of them when they set out, but they passed him and when they reached the port and looked back they saw his sails blowing wildly midway between them and Delos.

'Will he make it? He's a rotten sailor,' said Nicole, and Frazer shaded his eyes to stare at William's boat.

'He'll be all right, he knows these waters and he'll soon be in the shelter of the headlands and then the wind won't blow so hard.' He gave her a hand on to the jetty and followed her. Adoni greeted them smilingly. Frazer gave him some coins, patting his shoulder.

'Thanks, Adoni.'

Nicole walked on, scowling, and Frazer caught up with her. 'What was the money for?' Nicole demanded. 'Did Adoni spy on me again and run off to you to tell you we were going to Delos?'

'Adoni's a *friend* of mine,' Frazer said, then in an undertone: 'If you don't smile and look pleasant while they're all watching us I'll beat the living daylights out of you when I get you home.'

Nicole stiffened, but the hand under her elbow was biting into her flesh and his voice had the ring of certainty about it; she hurriedly cancelled her scowl and summoned up a happy smile.

Frazer nodded and spoke to most of the men they passed, who answered smilingly but whose shrewd black eyes watched Nicole as she walked past in a way which made her realise how much they saw. Rain began to splash down on them before they reached Frazer's house; they had to run the last hundred yards, but before she had got into the shelter of the courtyard Nicole's silvery hair was wet through and clinging to her scalp in fine strands.

When they were safely inside the house, Frazer shut the door on the wind and rain, facing her in the shadowy corridor, his lean body suddenly menacing.

'I thought I told you to wait for me to take you to Delos?'

'Since when did you give me orders?' Nicole asked, pushing back her wet hair from her face. 'I'm going up to my room to take a shower and get into some dry clothes.' She walked past him, expecting him to stop her, but he made no attempt to do so. It wasn't until she was halfway up the stairs that he spoke again.

'It can wait,' he said, and she felt a shiver run down her spine at the way he said it. She decided it was more dignified to ignore him than to turn round and yell the sort of things she wanted to tell him. That could wait too, she thought. She needed time to think up some suitable epithets, ones with real impact and bite, which would give him some insight into how she felt about him, although she could look ahead at years of doing just that, enlivening the long winter evenings of her life by inventing insults for Frazer Holt. Too bad he wouldn't be around to hear them; that was the one drawback to walking out of his life for ever, as she fully intended to do tomorrow.

She barricaded her bedroom door with every piece of movable furniture and then stripped off and took a leisurely shower. She didn't hurry about getting dressed again, either. By the time she had put on a pleated cream skirt and a warm pink sweater with a scooped neckline, the room was so dark that she had to put on the light. The storm still blew outside, the sky was lowering as though the weather had come to stay. It was hardly the perfect weather for sailing; she looked out of the window, frowning. Unless this storm blew out she wasn't likely to get away from Mykonos for a day or two.

There were still a lot of questions unanswered, of course, she would be returning to England without knowing the entire truth about Melanie's death, but suddenly she was tired of probing away and dragging out tiny details to fit into her picture of the past. It had all seemed so simple before she came here; she had been so obsessed with Frazer and how she felt about him that she had confused the two things. She had come here to find Frazer and punish him—but for what? She had told herself it was to punish him for what he had done to Melanie, but now she knew it was to punish him for what he had done to herself. Frazer had been right; if she kept on digging away all she would do was stir up mud which would stick on innocent people.

Now that she knew them all—Irena and her husband and Georgi Vourlamis—she found it impossible to believe that any of them had deliberately caused Melanie's death. They were all involved, that much was obvious, but if there was any guilt it did not belong to them. Who was she to accuse anyone of the guilt, anyway? Guilt for what? Melanie was dead, what good would it do to find out exactly why and how? She no longer wanted to know.

It took her five minutes to dismantle her barricade and put all the furniture back where it belonged, and when she got downstairs she found Frazer in the kitchen drinking brandy and watching the rain beating against the windows.

It was dark now, the room looked cosy and comforting compared to the weather outside, but Nicole felt cold as Frazer looked around at her.

'Pour yourself a stiff drink,' he said.

'Am I going to need one?'

'Oh, yes,' he said, and drank some more from his own glass, watching her walk across the room and pick up the bottle of brandy and a glass. She poured herself a finger of the spirit and stood sipping it, feeling the warmth of it circulating in her veins, but feeling even more the sting of Frazer's hostile stare.

'You wouldn't leave it alone, would you?' he erupted suddenly. 'Oh, no, you're the great detective—you had to keep on asking questions, prying into things that don't concern you, reminding people of things they preferred to forget. Can't you get it through your head? It was an accident, Melanie drowned by accident, nobody was to blame but her.'

'Then why wouldn't you tell me the whole truth? Why make such a mystery of it?'

He put down his whisky and walked across the room, then swung and walked back, both hands raking his hair.

'Damn you, Nicole, because people don't want to talk about something that doesn't give you the right to nag away until they tell you their secret!' He stopped in front of her, blue eyes angrily bright, his black hair dishevelled now. 'It's such a stupid, everyday little secret anyway, if you were as clever as you think you are, you'd have guessed by now.'

'Maybe I have,' she said. 'Maybe I think Georgi Vourlamis started some sort of fling with Melanie and it was him she went over to Delos to meet that night.' She watched Frazer's face, but it didn't tell her anything. 'Maybe I think it was an accident, she drowned and Georgi came over here to tell you, but as she was dead there seemed no point in admitting why she was on Delos, because that would mean a public scandal and Georgi might lose his job, not to mention his fiancée. So you told Georgi to keep his mouth shut and sent him back to Delos to wait for news, and then when Melanie's body was found you acted amazed and said you had no idea how she came to be on Delos but she'd gone swimming alone that night. Nobody took much interest because you were definitely here in Mykonos that night—I suppose you had an alibi, you were with someone. People saw you. You weren't suspected and the police just put it down as accidental death and forgot it. It was so much tidier.'

'Georgi hadn't committed any crime,' Frazer said tightly. 'Melanie chased him; he didn't chase her. He was bored and lonely, stuck over there with just a few other site workers around. She was bored, too, and she wanted to hit back at me for making her stay here. She used to get fishermen to drop her off at Delos in the afternoon and she'd stay there all night, sleep out on the beach, swim in the moonlight. It was becoming a regular thing with her.'

'Very romantic,' Nicole said with dry irony, but inside she was aching for Melanie. Had it seemed romantic? Swimming by moonlight on a deserted island beach? Delos was a magic place when the sun poured down that brilliant light, but it must be even more mysterious and haunting by moonlight.

'Georgi felt guilty, though—he knew it would get back to his girl sooner or later and he wanted to end it. He told Melanie that night, she mustn't come again; it was too dangerous. They had a row, he admitted that. He got dressed and was going to leave, but Melanie wouldn't get in the boat. She swam away from him when he tried to pull her into it. She was hysterical, she wasn't looking where she was going and she swam straight into a rock.

Georgi was too far away to get to her in time, by the time he did get there she'd vanished. When he realised she must be dead he came over and woke me up, and when I'd heard what had happened I decided there was simply no point in dragging all of us into the limelight. I told him to pretend he knew nothing about it. It seemed the simplest course of action. Next morning I told the police Melanie hadn't come home. They politely pretended to be surprised, but I guess they'd heard she was always with other men. When her body was washed up and her clothes were found on Delos there were a few questions, but it looked like an accidental death, nobody was suspected of having done anything criminal, so they dropped it.'

Nicole believed him this time, his tone was flat and matter-of-fact. She nodded. 'I only have one last question—why didn't you tell me all this days ago?' She smiled bitterly at him and didn't wait for him to answer, it was a rhetorical question she meant to answer herself. 'Because Irena asked you not to,' she said. 'That's right, isn't it?'

He nodded without seeming guilty or surprised. 'Obviously none of the Vourlamis family wanted an outsider to know about Georgi.'

'But it was Irena who mattered,' Nicole said. 'You lied to me about that, too, didn't you?'

Frazer stared at her, his brows black. 'Now what the hell are you getting at?'

'You and Irena!'

'Irena and me?' he repeated as though reversing the order of their names meant anything.

'I *know*, Frazer, there's no point in lying about that any more, either.'

His mouth tightened, hard and level. 'Isn't there?' he asked warily in a voice which gave nothing away. 'Can I ask exactly what it is that you *think* you know?'

'I don't think—I'm certain. You're having an affair with her, that's why you lied to me, that's why you seduced me, to stop me finding out about Georgi.' While she was spitting the words out she was struggling not to sound jealous or bitter or hurt, but she had a sinking feeling she was not succeeding; the emotions seething inside her were too strong to be hidden.

'Did I say you were clever?' Frazer muttered, staring at her with eyes like blue flint. 'I take it back. You're stupid, Nicole, you're probably the most stupid woman I've ever met.' While he was hurling that at her his voice was rising like the wind outside, full of fury. 'What in God's name makes you think . . .'

'I heard you!'

'Heard me?'

'On the phone.' She had to speak tersely, in a crisp sharp voice that threw words at him like hail rattling on a windowpane, because if she opened her mouth too wide the scream pressing against the top of her skull might escape.

'On the phone?' He looked at her blankly, as though regarding someone showing signs of incipient lunacy.

'Last night,' she said through her teeth. 'Last night, on the phone.'

'Last night on the phone?' Frazer repeated slowly, and that was too much—her temper burst like a cracking dam and her wild rage poured out, she almost screamed at him.

'Stop bloody repeating everything I say, you bloody parrot!' She knew why he was doing it, to gain time so that he could think of some plausible explanation, but he needn't bother, this time he wasn't sweet-talking her into believing anything he said.

He took two steps very fast, Nicole reacted with split-second timing, her brain so confused with fierce feeling that she leapt at him at the same instant, not in the coolly worked out posture she had been trained to take up but in spitting, clawing fury like a cat, her green eyes flashing.

She didn't get a chance to hit him. The next moment his arms were clamped around her body, forcing her own arms down at her sides within that iron ring.

'Don't touch me, I hate . . .' she began, and his mouth was suffocating her, ramming the words back into her, his own rage giving a consuming heat to the kiss he was inflicting on her. There was nothing loving or tender in the way he kissed her at that moment; he hurt her and meant to hurt her, he humiliated her and meant to humiliate her. She was helpless inside the rigid circle of his arms, however much she writhed and struggled she couldn't escape, and gradually her body went limp and her mind cloudy as the fumes of desire filled it, making it impossible to think.

Frazer lifted his head, breathing thickly. 'Does it have to be a goddamned fight every time I see you?' he muttered, staring down at her uplifted face.

She opened her eyes, trembling; green eyes drowsy and languid, her lips parted and moist, faintly swollen by the brutality of the kiss.

'Bastard,' she whispered, hearing the rapid thud of his heart, looking into the intent blue eyes and wishing she could use them as windows into that scheming head of his. What lay behind their stare? What sort of man was he? Why had she had to fall so deeply, destructively in love with someone who lied to her, cheated her, hurt her? And why didn't he kiss her again before she died of the sheer necessity of feeling his mouth on her own?

'I love you,' Frazer said with husky impatience, his voice so deep it seemed to be shaken out of his body.

'No,' she said, shuddering because she wanted it to be true so much and she knew he was lying.

'Yes, damn you,' he muttered, and kissed her again, one arm lifting to clasp her head, his fingers thrust through her fine, silvery hair, the wayward coils of it clinging to his skin. Electricity crackled inside her and although she was now free of the cage he had shut her into she made no attempt to escape, her mouth clung to his with hungry desperation because she was going away soon—she would never see him again, never kiss him again, and the realisation was agony.

She slid her arms round his neck and her hands stroked his nape, touched his thick black hair, fingered the strong muscles in his shoulder.

He took his mouth from hers, curved a hand round her throat and pushed her head back. Nicole unwillingly opened her eyes to look at him.

'I've never so much as kissed Irena,' he said. 'We aren't having an affair, we aren't in love—you're crazy, I don't know what you thought I was saying on the phone last night, but . . .'

'You told her you'd dealt with me, there wasn't any problem any more!'

'Did I?' He frowned. 'Well, what if I did? How does that make me her lover?'

'You plotted with her, the two of you planned . . .' she

swallowed, she couldn't put into words what she knew they had planned.

'Planned what? I promised Irena and Paul that Georgi wouldn't be dragged into any scandal about Melanie's death, that's all.'

'Did she suggest seducing me to keep me quiet? Or was that your idea?' She looked at him bitterly, with hatred, and Frazer looked back at her with widening eyes, his face hardening.

'So that's it!'

'That's it,' she muttered, her eyes hot with unshed tears.

'How far do you think I'd go to keep you quiet?' Frazer asked in a dangerously quiet voice. 'Marriage? Do you think I'd marry you to shut your mouth? That's what I told Irena on the phone—that I was going to marry you. Ring her—ask her. If you were listening you must have heard me tell her.'

She was shaken, staring at him, trying to read the truth in those deceptive blue eyes. 'I heard you laugh and say yes, you *were* clever, she was right.'

'What?' He gave a long, impatient sigh. 'I told Irena there wasn't a problem any more—and before I could explain Irena laughed and said she could guess why, she wasn't stupid, I was in love with you, wasn't I? And I said she was quite right, it was very clever of her, then I told her I was going to marry you as soon as I could talk you into it.'

Confused and uncertain, Nicole shook her head. 'No, you're lying again . . .'

'I've been in love with you ever since I first saw you,' he said harshly. 'In that street in Mallaig. You were everything I wanted in a woman, I couldn't take my eyes off you, if you hadn't been so young we'd have been married then.' He pushed her away violently. 'My marriage to Melanie was one long nightmare—I thought I'd put it all behind me until you reappeared and I rediscovered my dream woman, only this time you *were* a woman, not an adolescent who didn't know she was born. I took you to bed because I was dying to make love to you from the minute I saw you in that hotel bedroom. One look and it started again, but in a new way, the urgency was much worse this time.' He stopped, swallowing convulsively, his eyes dark. 'It's my bad luck that I'm crazy about a woman with a mind like a corkscrew!'

She felt her stomach sinking, she felt sick. She believed him, and she was scared by the bleak expression in his darkened eyes. Frazer had loved her and she had driven him away again, but this time she hadn't had any help from Melanie, she had done it all herself.

'Frazer . . .' she began shakily, searching for words to tell him how she felt, say how sorry she was, beg him to forgive her.

He stared at her fixedly without smiling, his bone structure clenched in that harsh bitterness, then suddenly without a word turned on his heel and walked out of the room, leaving her icy-cold and in despair.

She heard him running up the stairs, heard his bedroom door slam. Tears had spurted from her eyes, she couldn't stop crying, she couldn't see, blinded by the pain and misery which had taken hold of her. Outside in the dark night the rain rushed down the windows and the house was ominously silent.

Then she heard Frazer moving again, the crash of his feet on the stairs as he came back. She hurriedly scrubbed her hand over her wet face a minute before he burst into the kitchen.

'Where is it?' The snarl of his question made her jump nervously.

'Where's what?'

'The album.'

'Oh,' she said, flushing and feeling him watching her, knowing he must see the tear stains on her cheeks. She would have nasty little red eyes for a week, she thought, biting her lip. Looking down, she stammered: 'I'm sorry, I thought it might tell me something about Melanie. I know I had no right to search your room, I'm sorry . . .'

'You've seen it,' he said flatly, oddly.

She shook her head. 'Not yet, I haven't had a chance to . . .'

'Get it,' he snapped.

Nicole flinched and moved to the door. 'Yes, of course, I'm sorry.' If he had ever honestly loved her, he hated her now; she felt him withdrawn, remote, at a cold distance and it hurt.

She dragged herself upstairs wearily and found the album under the mattress where she had left it. When she got back to the kitchen with it Frazer was standing staring out of the rainwashed window with his back to her, and she wished she could think of something, anything, to say to placate him.

He turned and she wordlessly held out the album. He took it, staring at her. 'Looked at it now?'

She shook her head; she hadn't wanted to, she didn't want to see pictures of Melanie. Melanie was dead now, for her; the past was buried, but not before it had managed to destroy the present, and Nicole never wanted to think about Melanie again.

Frazer threw the album on to the table. 'Well, look at it now,' he said.

She looked down, her body cold and trembling. 'I don't want . . .'

'I don't give one damn what you want—I said look at it!' The ferocity of that made her jump with nerves and she didn't dare to argue any more, she turned and looked down at the album, opened it with shaking fingers and forced herself to look at the photographs it held. She saw herself.

Her body stiffened. She was so young; with a long, silvery plait of hair and a smooth laughing face, her long legs deeply tanned, her eyes looking out of the photographs with direct, open stare.

She heard Frazer breathing behind her, she turned the page and saw herself again, on a boat, Sam's boat, in a lifejacket, her hair whipping round her face, pulling on a rope and laughing. Then on the next page again there she was in jeans eating chips and sitting on a quayside, in shorts and a t-shirt leaning over the side of the boat and watching the wake stream behind on the blue water.

Page after page, the same; always herself, only herself. She looked at every one of the photographs and remembered him taking them, and felt a piercing happiness, an aching pain.

When she shut the book and looked round Frazer stared at her expressionlessly.

Nicole dared not move, she didn't know what to say or do, she was too frightened that she might do or say the wrong thing. She felt they were poised on a knife edge of possibility; if this moment was mishandled she might never see Frazer again.

'There isn't anything of Melanie left in this house,' Frazer said in a level voice. 'And she was never inside me—only you ever got to me like that.' He paused and she tentatively, uncertainly, held out a hand to him, her eyes dilated with intense feeling.

Frazer slowly took it and as they touched Nicole felt the tension break. She moved towards him and he moved towards her, and then she was in his arms and they were both talking, brokenly, incoherently, but now there was no distance between them, now they understood each other without fear or suspicion. 'I love you, I love you,' was really all they had to say. No other words mattered.

Harlequin Plus

A WORD ABOUT THE AUTHOR

Since she began writing for Harlequin Presents in late 1978, Charlotte Lamb has had close to forty books in this series published. Her explanation for this tremendous volume of superb romance writing is simple: "I love to write, and it comes very easily to me."

Once Charlotte has begun a story, the plot, the actions and the personalities of the characters unfold effortlessly and spontaneously, as her quick fingers commit the ideas of her fertile imagination to paper.

And so, in her beautiful old home on the rain-swept, uncrowded Isle of Man, where she lives with her husband and five children, Charlotte spends eight hours a day at her typewriter spinning loves stories — and enjoying every minute of it!

Her career as a writer has opened many doors for her, and travel is one of them. Yet despite all the countries she has visited and enjoyed in the past few years, her greatest love is still London, the city where she was born and raised.

Take these  best-selling 4 novels FREE

Yes! Four sophisticated, contemporary love stories by four world-famous authors of romance FREE, as your introduction to the Harlequin Presents subscription plan. Thrill to **Anne Mather**'s passionate story BORN OUT OF LOVE, set in the Caribbean.... Travel to darkest Africa in **Violet Winspear**'s TIME OF THE TEMPTRESS....Let **Charlotte Lamb** take you to the fascinating world of London's Fleet Street in MAN'S WORLD....Discover beautiful Greece in **Sally Wentworth**'s moving romance SAY HELLO TO YESTERDAY.

Harlequin Presents...

The very finest in romance fiction

Join the millions of avid Harlequin readers all over the world who delight in the magic of a really exciting novel. EIGHT great NEW titles published EACH MONTH! Each month you will get to know exciting, interesting, true-to-life people .... You'll be swept to distant lands you've dreamed of visiting .... Intrigue, adventure, romance, and the destiny of many lives will thrill you through each Harlequin Presents novel.

Get all the latest books before they're sold out!
As a Harlequin subscriber you actually receive your personal copies of the latest Presents novels immediately after they come off the press, so you're sure of getting all 8 each month.

Cancel your subscription whenever you wish!
You don't have to buy any minimum number of books. Whenever you decide to stop your subscription just let us know and we'll cancel all further shipments.

Your FREE gift includes

Anne Mather—Born out of Love
Violet Winspear—Time of the Temptress
Charlotte Lamb—Man's World
Sally Wentworth—Say Hello to Yesterday

FREE Gift Certificate
and subscription reservation

Mail this coupon today!

Harlequin Reader Service

In the U.S.A.
1440 South Priest Drive
Tempe, AZ 85281

In Canada
649 Ontario Street
Stratford, Ontario N5A 6W2

Please send me my 4 Harlequin Presents books free. Also, reserve a subscription to the 8 new Harlequin Presents novels published each month. Each month I will receive 8 new Presents novels at the low price of $1.75 each [*Total—$14.00 a month*]. There are no shipping and handling or any other hidden charges. I am free to cancel at any time, but even if I do, these first 4 books are still mine to keep absolutely FREE without any obligation. 108 BPP CACS

Offer expires August 31, 1984

NAME   (PLEASE PRINT)

ADDRESS   APT. NO.

CITY

STATE/PROV.   ZIP/POSTAL CODE

If price changes are necessary you will be notified.